First-time author David Slade at 60, will blow the minds of his childhood contemporaries. His headmaster had him destined for a very ordinary life on the end of a broom, but after a wide career that has seen him have the need for armed guards in Manchester and daily commutes to Scotland, it is his passion for arts and in particular writing which led him to write *The Third Tunnel* as a stage show during the early 2000s, with the Company of A Class Act Theatre in Newbury, David's hometown, staging the show on several occasions in the local theatres. David's mum and dad met at the local Corn Exchange during their pantomimes and his grandfather, a cockney who'd moved from London after the Blitz, would operate the Box Office at this time, David has theatre very much ingrained.

A Class Act Theatre Company (Newbury)

David Slade

The Third Tunnel

AUSTIN MACAULEY PUBLISHERS™

LONDON • CAMBRIDGE • NEW YORK • SHARJAH

A CIP catalogue record for this title is available from the British Library.

ISBN 9781398453616 (Paperback)
ISBN 9781398453623 (ePub e-book)

www.austinmacauley.com

First Published 2023
Austin Macauley Publishers Ltd®
1 Canada Square
Canary Wharf
London
E14 5AA

Caroline, Aimee and Beth Slade and the dogs.
A special thank you to Saffron Hewitt for the cover picture.
And to Catherine Freemantle for facilitating the picture.

"Oh blinkin' hell! not another one! These bloody nylons are useless. I've got two ruddy great big ladders in the left leg and three holes in the right and one of me toes is sticking right out."

"Ethel, will you stop moaning about your legs? You're bloody lucky you can get a pair of nylons to fit."

"Yeah well, you shouldn't be so abnormally long in the leg."

It was early evening and getting dark, soon, most of London would again be heading down into the tubes to escape another barrage from Hitler's bombers.

"It's been two weeks now and I ain't seen Ralphie outside the tube once. Do you think he's been nicked?" mused Ethel, a thirty-something, 'professional lady'. She had plied her trade all over London for the past decade and she had earned well but never having put anything away for a rainy day had cost her dearly of late. Hitler had warned Europe but had they taken any notice and now, every night for the past two weeks, herds of Heinkel's had appeared overhead at nightfall and dropped thousands upon thousands of pounds of scrap metal onto a once booming London's streets causing huge disruption, despair and downright inconsideration. As Ethel was now skint, she hadn't worked in weeks and her best night attire was now looking as if she'd had a visit from a horde of hungry moths. It didn't help that she lived in a very questionable flat close to Aldwych Station in Kemble Street near Drury Lane. Many of her customers had been the rich socialites that flooded into the area to see the shows at the many theatres that made up The West End. She was well known for her style of attracting men of all ages and fleecing these men out of their money, which had become her sole intention. But now with the advancement of Hitler's bombing campaign, the tourists had stopped coming to town at night and her earning capacity had taken a nosedive. The men she did attract, couldn't afford the high life with a night in one of the swanky hotels on The Strand. So they were often taken back to her flat, a dark and dank place on the first floor above an old shoe shop; the entrance to which was down a small dark alleyway which led to the rear of the building where an old brick staircase led you up to a front door which hadn't seen any paint since the turn of the century. Flat 31b had been Ethel's home for the last five years but since the start of the bombing, Peggy had been living with her. They both needed each other's company as the sight of the mass of swarming planes each night filled them both with dread and being together made life a bit more bearable. The flat was comfortably big enough for the two of them and they both had a room each to sleep in. Although Ethel's room was also her place of business, she tried to make it respectable with nice pictures on the walls and frills on her curtains but it remained what it was, 'her office'. Peggy never ventured in there. In the corner of the room was a large bed double in size but the 'bed' in which was so often pressed into action was no more than a straw-filled palliasse laying on an old rusty frame that resembled a barb-wired field enclosure and with no electric lighting in the flat, it was a daily occurrence that she would snag her clothing and now, she needed something new. Ralph, one of London's best-known Spivs, was the only person who could possibly get her out of this problem.

"You heading down the tube tonight, Peggy?" Ethel asked her new flatmate.

"Of course, I'm going down the bloody tube. Do you think I'm staying here to get me head blown off?" Peggy was similar in age to Ethel but had spent most of her life in and out of care until she was old enough to make her own decisions. At that point, she dropped out of society and started living rough on London's streets, mostly in the doorways of the big stores up west begging during daylight hours at the entrances to many of the underground stations in the centre of the capital. Whilst, of course, she was a gentle lady to many and in return, many saw her alright and kept her fed and watered and warm during the winter and with enough change in her purse, to buy a cup of 'rosy lee'.

"Alright, gal. Calm down, I was just asking. Look, I'm heading that way now I'm going to see if I can catch up with Ralph."

"What, that bloody spiv?" spat Peggy. She had a genuine mistrust of people like Ralph.

"Yes, that spiv bloke," replied a slightly peeved Ethel.

"He'll turn you over, no question," said Peggy trying her best to get Ethel to take her advice.

"No, I think he fancies me, so I'm going to give him some of that good ole Ethel cheek and before you know it, Bob's you uncle and Fanny's your aunt." Ethel stood up from the small seat she had perched herself on whilst adjusting her nylons, took a swig from her small silver flask, a present from a previous admiring customer and made for the door.

"Yeah, whatever. Look, I'll see you down there I need to

go and see whispering Harry to see if he's got any more of that brandy he had the other night. If I got to spend another night down on that rotten platform without a drink, I might as well stay up here and take me chances with the rats."

Walking up Drury Lane towards The Aldwych on her way to The Strand, which would take her in a big circle back towards The Aldwych looking for Ralph, Ethel felt particularly uncomfortable in her torn and tattered garbs. It was normal for her to wander this part of London at this time of day as she normally earned enough to keep her dressed as if she had just stepped off the pages of Tatler. Recently, however, she may as well have been promoting 'Farmers Weekly', she thought and she didn't like how this made her feel, but as she tried putting this to one side she had her eyes firmly peeled on each and every doorway. If Ralph was working tonight, his 'office', was usually one of the grand entrances along the Strand and right up to the tube station where Ethel, Peggy and many others were going to take shelter tonight.

Coutts was always one of Ralph's favourite locations as it made him feel he had a Royal connection and gave him some credibility with people from out of town. Tim was one of these out of Towners, dressed perfectly in his shooting breeks, flat cap and a beautifully polished pair of brown 'Full Oxford' brogues. All that was missing was a ditzy spaniel yapping wildly at his feet and a broken Purdy hanging from his arm. But tonight, he needed help and Ralph could spot the potential of someone not in the know from a mile off. This is what had given him his unsavoury reputation amongst the 'money' in that part of town even if nearly all the locals had benefited from Ralphs 'wares' at some time or another. The war might have been raging for quite some time now but if you wanted or needed it, Ralph had a way of laying his hands on it. A strikingly handsome man bedecked in what looked like a creation from Saville Row, but was more likely something run-up in the East End by one of the many tailors who could earn a pretty penny emulating Saville Rows finest for a fraction of the cost. Ralph stood tall in dark 'two-tone' spectator brogues, topped off by a very fine charcoal Trilby where he kept all the notes he dealt in. Tim wanted a shelter that night and for reasons only known to Tim, he had been led to believe he needed to buy a ticket to get to the platform tonight and Ralph knew this but, then Ralph knew everything on his patch and so as Tim approached, Ralph stood out from where he had stalked his prey.

"Tickets, anybody needs any tickets. I have tickets for all the best and safest parts of the station. You want a bed for the night, come and see Ralph." This was music to Tim's ears and so eagerly he approached Ralph.

"Well," said Tim, "I want to go as deep as possible."

"Deep as possible, eh? You regards yourself quite highly then?" replied Ralph in his best 'RP'.

"No more so than anyone else and I want a non-smoking environment."

"No smoking, eh?" said Ralph, slowly scratching his chin and pausing for the greatest effect. "Now that's not going to come cheap." Pausing a while longer, Ralph led with his first offer. "I think we should say 10 shillings, don't you?"

"And I think, we should say five and no more," Tim buffered. With this, Ralph turned his back and casually started to walk back up the Strand.

Stopping some yards away, slowly, Ralph turned to face

Tim. "You're staying in the Ticket Hall tonight then," Ralph said before moving on some more. Fearing a lousy night and no real shelter Tim upped his offer.

"OK, OK, I'll give you eight shillings but no more." Ralph sensed the kill was almost his, and so looking at his imitation Rolex, he paused for effect, shook his wrist until his watch disappeared under the sleeve of his elegant jacket.

Looking at Tim, Ralph said incredulously, "Twelve!"

Almost as if disbelieving the time shown on his fake kettle, "Ten then," said Tim and with that, Ralph grabbed his hand and shook it fervently and from the breast pocket of his suit, Ralph took a nice crisp but frankly deceitful station ticket. "Done," said Tim as he accepted the ticket with glee. "You were my son." Ralph strode off in the other direction, leaving Tim proudly turning towards the entrance to Aldwych Station.

Across the road, Ardle and Paddy, two itinerant Irishmen were taking a keen interest in Ralph's business acumen and how he had managed to fool what on the face of it seemed to be an upmarket client into purchasing a non-existent ticket to the underground.

"Do you see the fool over there, Paddy? He bought a ticket to go down the tunnel. What the hell did he do that for?" said Ardle the taller of the two men.

"He seems pleased with himself as well, maybe we should have a word him."

Ardle seemed concerned for Tim's stupidity but as both men had led a life of crime, his concern was shallow. "Oh leave the stupid fool alone, Ardle. You know the English are well known for being a bit thick. They're not like us at all. Besides, we need to keep our heads down. If they bloody catch us here, there'll be trouble and you know it." Both men kept their heads down as they moved off in the direction that Ralph had been taking, managing to keep themselves out of sight in the shadowy doorways.

Further up the long street, Ethel was making her way towards where Ralph had been working, occasionally she would catch a glimpse of herself in a shop window and would groan at her dismay at how she looked, stopping every now and again to try and adjust what was left of her once beautiful dress, into something more, in keeping with how she wanted her appearance. Nearing the station entrance, she spotted him and Ralph spotting her, made a dash for the nearest alleyway.

"Ralphie, Ralphie!" she called after him.

Stopping in his tracks, Ralph replied in a curt manner, "What do you want?" Ethel moved closer towards the stricken Ralph and tried to snuggle up into his suave torso.

"That's no way to talk to a lady," Ethel said.

"Listen, in case you have forgotten, ladies are usually refined," Ralph sneered at Ethel, not wanting to touch any part of her.

"I thought I was," purred an increasingly ardent Ethel. "You're always calling me treacle." She again tried to snuggle tightly into Ralph. Ralph stood back from Ethel and with a look of disgust, wiped his hands as if to clean them on the sides of his suit.

"That's 'cause you always look sticky, I mean, look at your 'air."

"You cheeky blighter. I used three weeks' worth of beer tokens on this, then the pigeons in Trafalgar Square shat on me 'ead. Would you believe it?" Ethel replied, clearly upset by Ralph's observations.

"Look Ethel, I'm a busy man what is it you want?"

"I need some new nylons, Ralphie, payment in kind."
"Payment in what?" Ralph couldn't believe even Ethel would
suggest such a thing.

"Now clear off before the rozzers come and get us both in
schtuck. You want nice looking legs, Ethel. I could do you a
couple of used kit bags, mind you, your thighs wouldn't fit in.
Ha-ha!" Her illusion of her and Ralph shattered once more.
She felt her cheeks starting to burn and so as a crowd of people
all gathered around the entrance to the tube station in
readiness for another night in the underground, an
embarrassed Ethel sloped off into the ticket hall in search of
Peggy and the promised drop of Brandy that was to keep them
both warm in the draughty old tunnels.

Gertie and Reenie waited patiently in the queue for the lift
down into the station. They had both travelled since earlier
that afternoon from the east end as Gertie's house had taken a
direct hit and had been completely demolished. Alby, her
husband, had been alone in the house that night whilst she had
spent the night keeping Reenie company in the Anderson
shelter in the backyard of her house near the Isle of Dogs.
About to take their turn in the lift, Reenie spied Alby, slowly
ambling up the Strand, dressed in just his underwear, a pair of
tatty long johns that looked as if he'd worn them to work in
the fields and an old string vest that had the contents of his
last two Sunday roast dinners still clinging into the fabric at
the front, shuffling heavily in his dirty black wellington boots.
Reenie called him over. "Poor lamb. He looks all dazed and
confused," joked Gertie.

"So would you if you had Hitler drop half a ton of scrap
iron on your drum?" Reenie reminded her.

"Ere look at him." Gertie pointed at Ralph, who was now doing some business with an old gentleman right outside the station's entrance.

"I don't like his sort at all," she said turning her nose up at Ralph.

"Where's he get all his gear from? You know, I 'aven't eaten a fresh egg for nearly two years now. Yet, I've seen 'im swap three of them stupid deep tunnel tickets for three fresh eggs, four times this week already," Reenie replied very vocally.

"Our Alby says you gotta steer clear of his sort. Oooh, oh, Alby, over here." Still looking extremely broken, Alby slowly realised that the girls were calling to him and shuffled over to where they were stood in the queue.

"It's no good Gert, Jerry had me last night."

Uncaring, Gertie looked at Alby and muffled, "I know." "Bloomin undignified, I didn't even get me trousers on!" Alby declared, disgusted at his predicament. Clearly, Gertie wasn't interested.

"So I heard," she said lamely.

Reenie had been closely studying Ralph while they had stood there waiting. "Look, there he goes again. That's two more eggs, he's just pulled out of his jacket."

Alby, deep in his own thoughts, was still muttering away to himself, "Bloomin place is a mess." But in a flash, he realised what Reenie had said and turning to face the charismatic spiv, Alby shouted loudly above the noise of the crowd so that Ralph could hear, "He's just pulled what out of his jacket? He's lucky to have a jacket. Eggs, is it? I'll give him eggs; don't he know there's a war on."

"Course, he does, that's why he's making money out of

17

people like us. Leave it, Alby." Gertie tried desperately to placate the raging Alby.

Alby was having none of it and strode towards Ralph, stopping just short, he resisted tugging at the spiv's lapels. "Oi Sunshine!" he yelled at Ralph who stood a good 12 inches taller than the old east ender.

"That'll cost you 10, Bob," Ralph joked.

"What will?" Alby was not in on the joke.

"Sunshine, me old china." An amused Ralph was playing with Alby.

"I'll give you me old china," Alby replied sternly.

"You still got some then?" asked Ralph.

"Don't you get clever with me, I'll take my belt off to you," said Alby struggling to find his belt where it should have been at the top of his trousers.

"Looks like you'll have difficulty there an all," said Ralph staring as Alby just stood there in his underwear. Gertie's patience was wearing thin and becoming increasingly incensed by Ralph she turned to Alby.

"Is he getting clever with you?" she said.

"I'll swing for him if he is." Reenie joined in, "What's 'is name? I'll report him to my husband, my husbands a copper!" she said, wagging her long index finger towards where Ralph was standing.

"Leave this to me," rapped Alby.

"Alby, you're making a fool of yourself. You've only got your underpants on," Gertie said trying to push Alby to one side so she could approach Ralph herself.

"Look, my friend," said Ralph trying to defuse the situation. "It looks like you're in a bit of a predicament, and I might be able to help. Ralph's the name, buy and sell

18

anything. You must be from Wapping?" he enquired.

"How do you know that?" Alby asked.

"'Cause they took a direct hit last night and you look like you lost everything. Am I right? And I reckon you might be in need of a little bit of my help." Reenie grabbed Alby and started pulling at his old vest.

"Alby, Alby. Don't hold back Alby, he needs a good lamping." She started flapping her arms wildly as Ralph stood back cowering from the deranged cockney.

"Look, I don't need this sort of hassle," Ralph said trying to pacify the situation.

"You want me help or you don't want me help. It's up to you, we've all got to make ends meet and I just 'appen to use my noddle a bit." Alby looked at the big fella, stood in front of them all and knew he wasn't going to win this one. Ralph took a step back eyeing the three of them cautiously.

"Come on, Alby," Gertie said angrily. "Let's get you back to Reenie's place, clean you up, get a pint of rosy down you and see if we can smarten you up a bit." An embarrassed Ralph slowly backed off down the street towards The Strand, upset at being dragged into such a scene, Gertie, Alby and Reenie turned in the other direction, it was going to be another night in the Anderson for them, Reenie stopped and took a long lingering look at Ralph as he sauntered off in all his finery.

"'Appen I could use my noddle a bit," she said to herself.

"I rather like the look of him bit young, but I like 'em that way! And after all fresh eggs are better than powdered. And my husband does little to provide in any department." She soon caught up with the others as they disappeared off towards Fleet Street in search of a bus that would take them back to Reenie's near The Isle of Dogs. Ralph took one last look over his shoulder at the three of them as he too disappeared off towards Catherine Street to see if he could make a bob or two in Covent Garden before everyone disappeared for the night. One of them had caught his eye. He'd need to think long and hard about that one.

Almost as immediately as the clock struck seven, a long, drawn-out hum was heard way out to the east. As the first wave of German Heinkels started their approach towards the capital, speculatively, the ack-ack could be heard starting way off in the distance as the first bombers started to open the doors under their aircraft to reveal the deadly payloads destined for the heart of the capital. As they started to cross the East End, the night sky over the docks suddenly lit up as the reflection in the clouds resembled a sunset on a balmy summers evening. Bells were heard ringing furiously from the fire engines as they raced across the capital and the acrid smell of burning timber hung heavily in the air.

***

"Cor blimey! They're starting early tonight! What happened to the bleeding sirens?" Ralph cursed to himself loudly as he wandered across one of the many bomb sites that littered central London on his way into work. Pulling his long blue silk handkerchief from his top pocket, he held it across his nose and mouth to shield himself from fumes that were floating on the evening breeze. Stopping to pick his way around a large pile of twisted metal, a little voice came back at him. He looked around and was shocked to see a small boy sitting on top of a pile of concrete.

"All the local ones got knocked out last night, Mister," Josey butted in.

Josey was the leader of a gang of street kids. At fifteen, he no longer felt the need to be tied to his mother's apron strings so he'd started a gang with a load of like-minded scruffy individuals, a bunch of chancers who could get by and fend for themselves when the going got tough. He'd found it easy to recruit others from all over London. As more often than not, their dads were away fighting and their mums had too many other younger children to worry about what they were getting up to all the time. Josey hailed from the East End but could normally be found up West especially since the bombing had started as his mum came up west to shelter with other mums in the tubes. And while they were busy helping or looking the other way, he and the others would sneak off and kick their heels around town looking for different things to do until it got too late. And then they would all find their way back down the tubes for the rest of the night. Many a time, had seen them get a few close calls when buildings they had been hiding in earlier had suddenly taken a direct hit when they'd left and so they usually went back to these sites the next day, dodging anyone who had been placed on guard to see if they could salvage anything and nick it for their own use and then sell it once they got home the next day. They lived on their wits; were scruffy, dirty and would sell their grandma to the highest bidder, but they were kind and considerate to each other, something which Josey had instilled in his gang from the off. So as not to attract attention as being a feral bunch, they all wore the obligatory gas mask box like a medal around their scrawny little necks and would proudly show them to anyone. If asked what was in their box, they would whisk the box off, open it up and show a gleamingly clean mask. 'We ain't dying for no Hitler' was usually written on the inside of each of their boxes.

"And what you doing around these parts at this time of the day, my son?" Ralph knew all too well that approaching kids in this part of town wasn't always a good idea, especially when he was carrying such a large amount of stock on him. He'd heard of some lads getting bumped off by the gipsies that came into the area, so approaching the boy with caution Ralph stopped in the open ground and spoke from where he was.

"Me mam's down the tunnel and me and me pals can't be arsed to spend another night with all them old codgers. Look if everyone's down the tube, who's looking after the streets? No, what I mean?"

Ralph chuckled. *Smart arse,* he thought to himself. "I know what you mean son, but this 'ere, is a man's world," said Ralph giving the lad a wave and moving on in the direction he had been going.

"What's a twit like you doing up here then?" Ralph stopped dead a swirl of dust blew up from the dry hard ground. Josey had completely thrown him with his last comment, and he needed to gather his thoughts. He looked around to make sure no one else was approaching that was likely to try and steal his gear and then he started to slowly move back towards the stack of rubble that Josey was sitting on.

"OK son. Where's your mates then? Let's see if we can make ourselves some rich pickings while London sleeps," Ralph asked in a menacing tone.

"You're on mister. Charlie, Four Eyes, Slimy, Knock

Knees. Get over 'ere all of yer." Josey stood up on the top of the pile calling out in all directions this unnerved Ralph and he half expected to see a bunch of itinerant gipsies running at him from all directions. Checking his pockets, he was suddenly transfixed to the spot, unable to move, he feared for his safety, but almost as soon as Josey had stopped calling, out of every dark corner of the bomb site, came a small child running, slowly at first, then turning into a fast sprint as they neared where he was standing. Gathering around Ralph they started checking him out; looking at his shoes his hat and coat. Each time nodding their approval like an officer inspecting his troops. When they finished checking Ralph out, they immediately stood back gathering around Josey as if he were their commanding officer. Knock Knees, a small grubby fella with bandy legs, wearing an old grey sleeveless jumper with no shirt and a pair of grey flannel shorts that looked like the arse was hanging out of, looked Ralph up and down. All the while sniffing as if he had a cold, it seemed he had a bad habit. Lifting the hem of his jumper up to meet his running nose, he smeared its contents along the bottom of his jumper and then using the palm of his hand, wiped his nose in an upwards direction looked at what residue was there and then dried his hands on the front of his shorts.

"Who's the idiot in the hat then, Josey?" he said between sniffs. They all started firing questions randomly about Ralph.

"What makes his face so important he has to have his nose underlined?" asked Slimey, pointing at Ralphs elegant moustache.

"You a spiv? Or you dressing like that for charity?" asked Knock Knees, again checking out Ralph's two-tone brogues. "Funny bunch, your mates, ain't they!" said Ralph. Unnerved by the situation he found himself in, not sure whether to run or hide from a possible attack from some marauding youths on his 'goods' or to stay and have a laugh with a bunch of goofy kids, he kept his eyes peeled and joined in with the banter.

"You ain't very good looking, are you? That why you didn't get called up? A beret would look stupid on your 'ead." Four Eyes was one of only a few females in Josey's gang. A glasses wearer since she was a tiny tot, her nickname was easily earned so was the occasional slap her mother would give her thighs when she came home after breaking another pair. She wasn't so much a tomboy like some of the other girls as she still liked to play with her dolls when she was at home, something she kept from the gang, but she was kind when someone got hurt firing a catapult, or when they had stone fights with other gangs, so she'd become a good and trusted member of the gang and was always there when they needed her. Ralph took a long draw on a Capstan, full-strength cigarette, he'd lit during the exchanges and slowly exhaled a cloud of white smoke.

"Look you lot," he said seriously, "One rule and one rule only. Cut the cheek, I'm the boss, and if the rozzers come, you don't know me, got it?"

Charlie, was quick as a flash. He saw himself as the brains of the gang and would often question Josey on the things he had them doing. A West End boy with 'respectable' parents, business people, his dad ran a millinery shop not far from Covent Garden which served the high-class clientele. He was usually immaculately turned out at the start of any meetup. But after climbing through burnt-out windows and over bomb-damaged houses, his trousers or shirts were always getting torn and in turn, he would earn a good thrashing from his mum or dad when he got home.

"You didn't do well at school then, cos that's three rules!" he told Ralph in an educated way.

"One rule son, one rule." Ralph wagged his finger at them all, defiantly letting them know it was his way or not at all.

"'Ere you from around these parts then, Mister?" quizzed Josey from atop his stack. "Cause all the local spivs have been locked up."

"I move around a bit," Ralph told them. "You know keep on me toes," he said as he moved from side to side to indicate what he meant.

"Can you get anything we need?" Four Eyes asked. "Cos I'm starving." Ralph tried to breathe in, his own waistband had been expanding lately from all the chocolate he'd munched on, which made him suddenly feel somewhat guilty as the poor girl obviously hadn't had much in her tiny stomach for a while.

"Look if it's a good meal you're after, I'll see what I can sort, OK?" he said to her with a genuine look of pity in his eyes.

"OK but what about me 'ma?" *Hold up* he thought to himself, *I can't feed every waif and stray.*

"She good looking?" he tried to make a joke of it but the small girl didn't seem to get it.

"Leave it out, Four Eyes, so what you got planned for tonight then, mister?" asked an excited Josey as he climbed down from the top of the stack, indicating for Ralph to follow him a few yards from the others.

"You seriously think this gang of yours is up to my kind of work then mate?" Ralph half-whispered to Josey, normally he only had himself to worry about could he trust a bunch of chancers.

"Well, they don't have to know our motives," said Josey brazenly. Ralph gave it some thought

"OK," he said. "We'll test them. Get all your mates together and meet me on the corner of High Holborn and Kingsway in half an hour."

"No problems, Mister," Josey proudly declared.

Ralph shook the boy's grubby mitt, turned and started to shuffle off in his distinctive way in the direction he had been heading. Chuckling away to himself, he passed off Josey's boasts as nothing more than a backhanded juvenile show of strength, the children all looked on waiting for him to disappear before anyone said anything.

"He's weird. We shouldn't trust him, Josey. We'll only get into trouble. Your mam would have kittens if she knew we'd been out with him." Slimey's thoughts echoed most of the others stood there in the gloom of the evening's sunset.

"We could get into serious trouble with him Josey, it's not worth it. Why bother knocking about with some old geezer, we have enough fun on our own," argued Knock Knees. Josey thought for a while about everything they had said.

"Look, come on, let's give him a try. We can always clear off if it looks like things are getting out of hand, besides we just may have a bit of fun at his expense, know what I mean."

Anything Josey said would normally have had the gang whooping with delight at their next adventure, this time however, they were more subdued and unsure, they'd all been told to be wary of strangers and Ralph was weird as well, deep in thought nobody said anything.

Slimey suddenly spotted their nemesis out of the corner

of his eye, PC Selby, Reenie's better half, a copper, The Fuzz, Rozzers, call them what you like. Josey and his gang were always being collared by one of them, usually the copper gave them a small clip around the ear, which didn't hurt, and then sent someone round to their house the next day to have a word with their mum. But PC Selby was different, he was nasty and used to pull and twist their ears till they would scream and their ears would go bright red, stinging for ages after he let go. He was known by the kids as sadistic plod, when he couldn't hear them or close up, he was known as PC Challenge because he had enormous ears that resembled the handles on footballs FA Challenge Cup. The PC had been a copper for as long as he could remember, he always took his job seriously if somewhat obtusely especially where kids were concerned. Probably on account of Reenie's refusal to give him any but he was well known in the area, never a day went past without him pacing his beat proudly, claiming to keep all unlawful activity on his patch to an absolute minimum and he claimed it was only those times he was at home trying to keep the peace between him and Reenie that anything underhand would happen. Making out, he hadn't seen the children, he shone his torch up into the night sky and then flicked it around all the crooks and crannies of the upper parts of the buildings that surrounded them trying to look as if he was more interested in the stars or anything other than them.

They all huddled tightly together so that the copper couldn't hear them.

"Alright Josey," said Slimey. "We'll give him a go, but be on your toes. Let's all be on our toes. Blinkin rozzers are over there."

"All right, let's meet up again in half an hour. Now scarper!" ordered Josey. Quick as a flash, they all scattered off in the direction they had come from. Ralph watched them from afar until the dust they kicked up settled down again and with a smile to himself turned and carried on towards his first stop of the evening 'Jewish Ken'. He could always get a new supply of nylons from him and the profit he could make up west on them was worth the trip. It was a long way and he had to get back to see the kids in half an hour but if he caught the number 8 at the bottom of Longacre, he could just about do it in time.

None of them, not even the beady-eyed copper had spotted Paddy and Ardle lurking in the shadows.

"So he's got his claws into the kids now. I don't like this man at all, Paddy. We're going to have to keep an eye on the fellow, especially if we're going to make us a bob or two," Ardle whispered into Paddy's ear from their perch up in the damaged building next to the bomb site. They'd been tailing Ralph and had zig-zagged around the site when he was stopped by the children. They'd managed to get into the building opposite by pulling off some old metal sheeting that had been put over one of the doors, from there they'd gone immediately to the first floor and watched what had been going on from one of the blown-out windows.

"I'm on to it Ardle, you just concentrate on what you got to do," Paddy whispered back.

"Well don't you let me down Paddy, this little trip of ours has already cost me after that incident with the boat Paddy."

"It just wasn't big enough Ardle," Paddy told the Irishman seriously.

"For what Paddy?"

28

"To make a bridge," he said again in a serious tone.

"But it was a boat, Paddy."

Ardle implored rolling his eyes skywards towards the simple-minded Irishman. "That it was Ardle, that it was."

***

The early evening train, full of weary passengers, was rattling its way through the tunnels of the Piccadilly line on its way to dropping them all safely at their destinations. As it burst into the light of the station concourse at Aldwych, a horrified Winnie caught a glimpse of the young children in her charge all playing aimlessly on the platform edge.

She screamed at the top of her voice, "I told you, to get away from the edge you little bleeders!"

Scattering wildly in an instant, the children all ran back from the platform edge to the relative safety against the back wall of the station and huddled tightly against its green and white shiny tiles. Winnie was a blunt-talking cockney who had been sheltering down in the tunnels ever since the bombing started. Every evening, she would find herself a nice place to bed down and make the spot her own in typical fashion barging others out of the way. She would make it nice and warm and surround herself with her friends and neighbours along with her long-suffering partner Charlie. Charlie was another no-nonsense Cockney dressed in a flat cap old brown cords a white shirt with no collar and his old neighbour's black waistcoat he'd taken from his washing line the night he'd got bombed and hadn't survived. He smartened the outfit up with a gold chain he'd had since he was a kid, with a large pocket watch slung on the end it dangled from one pocket to the other in a gentle arc across Charlie's small paunch. Charlie's rough appearance belied his age. He should have been called up by now, but, until they did his conscience told him, that he was not sure whether or not war was something he could embrace.

Looking up and down the platform, Charlie eyed all the children "'Ere Winnie, where's young Josey? If he's gone walkabout again, I'll take my belt off to him, so help me." Charlie stood and tugged at the thick leather belt he had pulled tightly around his middle.

"Leave him alone, Charlie. Poor boys getting sick and fed up with all this bombing. He don't know if he's coming or going at the moment." Winnie leant back and craned her neck up and down the platform giving it a cursory look before going back to the conversation she was having with a friend sat next to her.

"He'll know if I get my hands on the little rascal. You know he was seen going up that tunnel the other night," said Charlie, nodding his head off into the distance.

"What tunnel?" Winnie said, tutting to herself that Charlie had disturbed her once again.

"Cor blimey, Winnie, that tunnel." Charlie had crouched down to Winnie's level and was pointing off in the distance.

"But there's three tunnels, Charlie," she said.

"That tunnel over there! See." Charlie reacted angrily to Winnie's ignorance, standing so he could be heard by everyone close by he spoke in a loud sarcastic way, "And they're worrying about deep tunnel mentality. I've had to put up with your mentality for years." He laughed along to his own joke, having seen something written about 'deep tunnel mentality' on a poster in the station's entrance. He looked around at all those present hoping they would join in, but they all remained silent so Charlie started to sheepishly fold his blankets ready for a good night's sleep.

"Oh Charlie, leave the boy alone. He was probably only investigating," Winnie added barely looking at him as she was still deep in conversation with the old woman.

Further along, the platform among the hordes of people all huddled shivering in the cold damp conditions were Connie and Alice, two young ladies from a different social class to many of those around them, Connie or Lady Constantine as she was known upstairs in the real world and Alice her regal partner. They had their country residence requisitioned and so they'd made their way into central London to stay at Connie's Mayfair home just as the bombing had started. So they now found themselves having to shelter with the rest of London down in the underground system far from the finery of their usual existence.

Having found a nice gap to make themselves a bed for the night, with what they hoped would be some 'nice' people they caught sight of Charlie and Winnie's bickering.

"What do those two think they're doing, shouting, and hollering at each other?" Alice said in a pompous voice.

"I know, Alice," Connie answered whilst looking down her nose at the squabbling cockneys. "He shouldn't be in here, do you know I was over at Covent Garden the other day and there was a poster on the wall which read, 'To all able-bodied me'."

"Well his sort doesn't look very able," Alice jumped in much to their amusement.

"It said, 'To all able-bodied men'. The trains must run to get people to their work and to their homes. The space at the tube stations is limited. Women, children, and the infirm need it most. Be a man and leave it to them," she finished.

"Well," said Alice, "he doesn't look like a man; my Alfred would make mincemeat of him."

Chuckling to herself, "Well, tell him to hurry up. I'm tired of eating Offal." They both fell about laughing and sniggering like two young schoolgirls.

"Here Connie, why don't you give us all a jolly good time, sing us one of your songs that'll cheer us all up. It's miserable down here and if we're to spend all night in here with that lot, we could do with some entertainment," Alice told Connie when they'd gathered themselves from their attempt at humour.

"You must be joking, that lot would think. No, it would be too embarrassing. They would think we're a couple of right idiots. I mean they haven't spoken to us all week, and we could find ourselves in the Anderson shelter at the bottom of your Grand mama's back yard if that lot had their way. No, no I couldn't." Disagreeing with her friend, Alice rose from her seat and shook her long gown so it hung perfectly just over the top of her black laced boots. Coughing to clear her throat, Alice stood as if to address the station concourse. First, though she looked down at the clearly embarrassed Connie, who was hiding her reddened face in the centre pages of The Times newspaper weekend edition, Alice wagged her finger at her and told her that she was talking nonsense as she was a fine singer who had graced some of the finest stages.

Connie begged her friend to stop and not do whatever it was she was about to do but ignoring her pleas, Alice took a deep breath faced the assembled group and shouted at the top of her voice, "I say, hello, hello. Can I have everyone's

32

attention?" Connie sharply tugged at Alice's exquisite Chanel dress and told her, in no uncertain terms, to sit down as she was making fools of them both. Ignoring her friend's desperate plea, she carried on, "I say, shut up, down there. Thank you. We have here amongst our midst."

Back along the tunnel, Winnie had been flapping since her disagreement with Charlie. She immediately stopped what she was doing as she caught sight of Connie and Alice making a disturbance and turned her nose up in disgust. She'd bumped into the two girls literally whilst waiting for her turn to get into the lift at street level and had sneered at the pair dressed in all 'their finery'. Charlie had thought differently and hadn't been able to keep his eye off the 'small one' as he'd put it when she'd overheard him talking to some other men about them when they'd got to platform level and she wasn't about to have them disturb her night or her little corner of London that she was so fiercely protecting.

"Who the blooming hell is that? Charlie, Charlie!" Winnie grabbed Charlie's shoulder as he lay snuggly on his blanket next to where she was sitting.

"What do you want now?" he said, "I'd just got me 'ead down." Weakly lifting himself up to try and see what all the fuss was about.

"Charlie…who's that making all that racket over there?" Tugging at Charlie and pointing her finger in the general direction of where the two socialites had made their bed. In no mood to have his sleep disturbed, Charlie collapsed back onto his comfy old blanket.

"Ow the bleeding hell should I know? I was asleep!" he said as he rolled back into the comfort of his makeshift bed.

"Well," said Winnie, "instead of whining about it. Get

your lazy good for nothing backside off of the floor and go and find out." Barely lifting his head up off the trousers he'd rolled up tightly to make a pillow Charlie told her sharply that he wasn't whining, he didn't care as he was 'asleep'! "Call yourself a man!" She barked back at him. Clearing her throat, Winnie stood up from the old orange crate she had been sitting on and struck up a mock posh accent, much to Charlie's amusement. "I say, I say, girls, what is it you want?" Charlie corpsed as he heard Winnie mockingly shout across the station at the girls in the distance. "Bleeding hell, Winnie! You got a problem with your north and south," he humoured as he tried to regain his composure.

"Shut up, Charlie!" She snapped back, slapping her hand down across Charlie's shoulder making him wince, as she called out to the girls again mocking their posh accent, "Girls?"

Mortified that Alice had upset any of those they were sharing the tube with, Connie stood apologetically and called out towards them all. "Sorry about my, about my so-called friend," she said. "Your so-called friend's making more noise than Hitler's bleeding bombers," Winnie answered quickly in her harsh cockney brogue, cheering wildly the crowd around her all pointed at the girls and pushed their noses into the air snootily.

Undeterred, Alice rose from her seat and shuffled through the throng of people towards the smug crowd of East Enders. Climbing over a few people who were by now asleep on the platform she made her way over to Winnie and tried to make the Cockney's acquaintance, holding out her hand in anticipation that Winnie would greet her with a warm handshake.

However, Winnie totally ignored Alice's outstretched hand and so the lady spoke to her in her warm aristocratic tone, "I do believe we haven't been introduced. Her Ladyship over there is Constantine, Connie to you, and me and I'm... I'm, well, I'll tell you what, just call me Alice."

Winnie looked the socialite up and down and started to circle around the elegantly presented lady. She ran her hand up and over Alice's beautiful cotton and silk dress. "Well," she said sneeringly. "What 'ave we got here then?" baiting the unfortunate Alice.

"Winnie!" Charlie barked cross that she was causing a stir again.

"Well, Charlie, it looks like we got some royalty here." As she curtsied scornfully to the young women.

"Oh we're not royalty, we were lucky to be born into good stock and since our country residence has been requisitioned!" Connie shouted, butting in from further back down the platform.

"We've..." She nervously looked over towards Alice for some support.

"How do you say it?" Alice shrugged her shoulders. "Pitched up here, in London." Trying to make her excuses before Alice embarrassed them further.

"Well, my girl, if it's a bed for the night you're enquiring about, I would love to have you tucked up here with me," Charlie offered cheekily tapping the makeshift bed he was lying on to show Connie where she could sleep much to the delight of all the men on that part of the station.

A little smile came across Connie's lips. "Well no, I just couldn't after all what would your lovely lady say."

"Say? Say? I wouldn't say nothing. But he'd get the back

of me hand, a bit sharpish an' all," Winnie hollered over to Connie, letting her and everyone else who could hear how she felt, before again cuffing Charlie sharply across the top of his back; appalled at his suggestion that the two of them should get together.

"My friend is a singer. A very good singer. Actually, she's been on stage at Drury Lane. And I thought we could all do with some entertainment." Once again Alice interrupted trying to cut the growing tension between the two groups.

Peggy, who had settled into a drunken stupor towards the back of the station platform, well-oiled from all the brandy she and Ethel had consumed after her visit to whispering Harry, was jabbering away to anyone who would listen about her life on the streets, trying to relieve them of the odd coppers she needed for a cup of tea during the day, heard Alice's request for entertainment and immediately shot to her feet.

"My old man says, follow the van and don't dilly-dally on the way," she drunkenly shrieked at the top of her voice, wobbling to and fro, using the wall to keep her upright. The entire station suddenly rounded on the poor unfortunate bag lady.

"Shut it!" Peggy stopped immediately and slid down the arched wall into a heap at Ethel's feet, snoring loudly much to the amusement of all those gathered in that area.

"OK. Let's put this another way, can any of you sing?" Shouted Connie, following Peggy's amusing performance. "For instance, let me try this one." Suddenly, everyone's eyes were on the posh lady who was standing in the middle of the platform.

"Oh dear," she muttered nervously to herself. "What have I said?"

"Come on then, what you waiting for!" someone quipped from further down the platform.

"OK," she said, steadying herself nervously her throat drying rapidly. Without music to back her, Connie began to sing. She had chosen to do a beautiful version of Vera Lynn's 'Lovely Weekend' and Charlie was transfixed the moment she started singing. Unable to take his eyes off the beautiful woman, he stood in silence until she finished. The platform of people launched into a rapturous round of applause as she finished and those close to Connie shook her hand and patted her on the back warmly. Alice looked across at her relieved friend and gave her a nod of approval and a knowing smile before Connie sat back down on her makeshift bed.

Now an impromptu party had started, Charlie sure of his own talent couldn't wait to keep things going, and so he called over to Peggy, who was still quietly embroiled in her own stupor at the back of the platform.

"Come on, love," he called to her. "Let's show 'em how it should be done!" Pulling Peggy to her feet, the pair threw themselves into a riotous version of 'My old man says follow the van'. Out of tune, the pair jigged from side to side gaily as the platform suddenly came alive. All the Londoners joined in the song and danced around their beds until they could sing or dance no longer.

Winnie, who had been chuckling away to herself and tapping her feet whilst mouthing the words turned to Charlie, when he'd finished and had managed to prop the still groggy Peggy back against the station wall, she shouted across. "Blooming hell, Charlie boy. What's all that about?" she said curled up with laughter.

"You wanna go steady or your Chalfont's will end up

splattered all over the bleeding platform if you ain't careful."

Adjusting his belt and tucking in his shirt, gasping for air, Charlie laughed at her indiscreet observation as he made his way towards the station's exit.

"You leave me farmers out of this; I'm starting to enjoy me self. Mind you, I think I need to shake hands with the vicar," he called back as he disappeared up the long winding stairway leading back to the surface.

Back at street level, Tim visibly chuffed to have managed to procure his ticket from Ralph for the non-existent part of the underground station approached the station concourse proudly, his ticket tightly gripped in his hand, as Victor, the station manager approached him. Victor had been an underground rail worker since he'd left The Queens Regiment, following the end of World War I. He'd won several honours with colours for his service in The Somme and had been a daily fixture at Aldwych station for years following his promotion to manager.

"What you got there then, son?" he asked Tim in his usual friendly warm manner. Tim who was still beaming from his earlier 'deal' with Ralph, pointed over to where he'd made the transaction with the spiv.

"It's my deep tunnel ticket. I just bought it from that gentleman over there…" his voice trailed off as he realised that no one was standing where he was pointing. Ralph had, by now, scuttled off into the distance and was nowhere to be seen.

"Oh, well, he was there a minute ago," he said, dismissing Ralph's disappearance. "He said he was selling tickets for this station so I asked him for a deep tunnel non-smoking environment. Which, I have just paid 10 shillings for. It was

38

a done deal, now go away young man and leave me to find my own way."

Neither young nor about to allow Tim to go into the station without him knowing the error of his way, Victor explained that the platform was free and was on a 'first come first served basis'.

"But he said," argued Tim.

"London's full of them," Victor said, trying to get Tim to realize that he'd actually been conned by Ralph.

"Wonderful!" Tim said, hardly able to contain himself. "I've been done…by a spiv! And being from out of town, can you imagine the story I can tell. I can dine out on this for months."

Charlie appeared at the top of the long spiral staircase in a hurry, his legs clamped ever so slightly together, running towards Victor like a penguin at feeding time. Desperately, he yelled over to Victor enquiring where the nearest toilet was, pointing off into the middle distance to the right of where they were standing Victor indicated that a toilet has been built further along The Strand from the station entrance. Charlie eyed the portable contraption with some trepidation, its corrugated sides and roof of rusting tinwork and sand bag protection piled around all four sides, didn't look at all very private let alone safe.

"Does it work?" he asked Victor nervously.

"I've just been had by a spiv," Tim butted in as Charlie stood there in obvious need of a call to mother nature. "Congratulations, son," said Charlie, showing no interest in Tim at all.

"But don't you think it's wonderful that at the height of the war, the good old British entrepreneurial spirit still shines through," an animated Tim gushed. Charlie stood stock still as he scowled at the 'idiotic' man in front of him. Desperately trying to control his muscles whilst chewing on the remnants of some treat he'd managed to purloin from some cheery chap on the platform, holding his breath as he turned a deep shade of red the more, he stood waiting to relieve himself. Victor smiled and shook his head at the picture before him, he decided to step in and save the desperate man.

"I wouldn't go there, mate," he said screwing his nose up and pointing at Tim. Charlie wasn't least bit interested in what the idiotic person had to say, he was 'bursting for the toilet'.

Victor took hold of Charlie's shoulders and turned him to face in the direction of the hastily built toilet, giving him a small push. Charlie scurried off quickly in the toilets' direction.

"By the way, I'd whistle as there's no lock," Victor called after him with a chuckle.

Tim still stood in the station's entrance, gripping his non-existent tunnel ticket firmly in his well-manicured fist, looked towards the toilet. "It looks a bit flimsy," he said to Victor. Biting back sharply, Victor barked at Tim "The sewerage ain't working down in the tunnels so we had to quickly build this up here."

"Well," Tim said, "if Hitler drops a bomb on it, you aren't going to be very safe in there, are you?"

Keen to rid himself of his nuisance, Victor was quick to explain that, "When half of London has been in there, you don't want to hang around long enough for the flies to land on you let alone one of Hitlers one hundred pounders." Suddenly, a huge explosion boomed out further down The Strand. The blast completely knocked both Tim and Victor off their feet, dumping them unceremoniously in a heap further back along The Strand. For a second, there was a deafly silence, as a pall of smoke and dust rose up from the ground around the makeshift toilet, Tim and Victor stumbled around briefly as they tried to extricate themselves from their predicament. Charlie emerged from what was left of the toilet, his trousers down by his ankles, a toilet seat neatly slung over his head and a long roll of toilet paper flowing behind him as he staggered around the curb side.

"Bleeding hell, Jerry!" Charlie yelled towards the heavens. "Can't a man even have a tom tit in peace!" Furiously, he shook his fist at the night sky.

"Blimey!" laughed Tim incredulously. "What a story!" Victor caught Charlie's eye as they both yelled at the hapless Tim.

"Shut up!" they screamed as Tim casually strolled back into the station's entrance and made his way towards the stairway which led down into the depths of the capital for an evening's costly shelter.

Paddy and Ardle had, by now, moved into the doorway of the building opposite to the entrance of the tube station. They had an excellent view undetected by Victor, Charlie, or Tim of what had been going on.

"See, I told you Ardle, they're all bloody thick!" Paddy mused almost falling off the step he was standing on.

For at least an hour, the relentless bombing of the capital had been underway and as the belly of the fires throughout London lit up the night sky and the massive beams from the searchlight stations danced across an inky black sky, many of the capital's residents fearing for their lives were by now sheltering under or inside whatever they felt safe in and the

Tunnels of the London underground were no exception. Hordes of people from all over London were, by now, deep in the underground tunnels, all trying to keep warm and forget what was going on outside, hoping and praying that when given the all-clear they still had a home to return to. All except for a small gang of wily children who had a special meeting to attend and so as Josey and his friends wandered along Kingsway in the direction of the planned meet, a tall statuesque figure that was the epitome of good looks and suave sophistication was already stood leaning against a boarded-up window some yards in from the corner of Kingsway and Queen Street, having raced back there from his meeting with 'Jewish Ken' to load up on some more stock of nylons and chocolate. Ralph was the kind of man who could smell an opportunity to make money three streets away and he had that feeling again deep in the pit of his stomach, Josey and his bunch of ragtag street kids were about to give Ralph another big payday.

As they moved towards where Ralph was standing, a huge explosion detonated off towards where they had been heading and almost simultaneously, the shockwave from the bomb tore into the street although not as strong as some they had felt due to the high buildings that surrounded this part of town but it was still enough to knock several of them of their feet. "Whoa! That was a bit too close!" yelled Josey as parts of brickwork and masonry fell into the far end of the street exactly where they had been due to meet with Ralph. Letting out a huge shriek, as she scrambled to her feet, the youngest member of the gang, Jenny, a small bespectacled grubby little child who hadn't washed since the water main in her street had taken a direct hit a fortnight earlier.

"Crickey Josey! Two more minutes and we'd have been in Jerry's sights!" she screamed, picking herself back up and wiping some dust off her small round wire glasses,

Ralph, who had ducked out of sight as he saw them wander down the street, had been lucky and missed the explosion by yards, watched all the commotion and noise they had been making and causally sauntered over to the gang of youngsters.

"You lot can certainly make one hell of a racket. Where we're going, you got to be quiet, you got that. OK?" Taking a huge draw on a Capstan full-strength cigarette, he adjusted the brim of his trilby and made sure his jacket was fastened just so and headed off in the direction from which Josey and all the other children had come. Slowly, one by one, they all fell into line behind him like the pied piper and his pilgrims as they all headed off towards Aldwych.

As they approached the southern end of the street, Ralph suddenly stopped, took another draw on his cigarette and causally nodded towards an opening within the wall, making sure as he did, so that no one else was watching. "This is what I wanted to show you," he said.

"There ain't many people know this exists. It's an old tunnel entrance that was last used back in the twenties when you kids were still just a glint in your old man's eyes. Down 'ere leads to tunnel three, not far from where your mums and dads are kipping down. It's dark, wet and it's got rats running all over the place. But stick with me and I'll show you some treasures you wouldn't believe. You gotta be dead quiet, and you don't nick nothing. You keep your hands in your pockets, you understand. This is more of an adventure."

Josey and his mates were normally a wary bunch

43

especially around adults but after a quick discussion amongst themselves, this seemed too much fun to resist. After all, an adventure under the capital, out of sight of moaning adults could reap a lot more than standing around street corners dodging Hitler's ammo.

Pulling back on a length hoarding to open up the entrance, Ralph stood to one side allowing the group of youngsters to peer in. As Knock Knees took his turn to gawp into the darkness, he looked at Ralph. "Have you bin' down ere nicking then, Mister? My dad reckons you're a thief, so does Aunty Vi," he said, but Ralph quicker than your average adult, immediately countered the small boy's cheeky enquiry.

"You ought to tell your mum to keep an eye on your dad and Aunty Vi." His reply brought a deafening silence as it flew over the children's heads, even if the bombing was still going on around them in earnest. Charlie Junior took his turn and peered into the doorway. Immediately, he jumped back, frightened by the darkness, he asked Ralph if he had any torches?

"Just leave the thinking to me, son," Ralph replied as they all started to disappear into the gloomy darkness of the entranceway.

Whilst they had all gathered around the old entranceway, waiting to take their turn to slip through the small gap, Ralph had strained his eyes in all directions. But on this occasion, he had been less than his usual diligent self as he had failed to notice that Paddy and Ardle had been tailing him from when he last met the children and that they had been stood across the street in a building that had been badly damaged some nights previously. From their vantage point, they could see and hear all that had been said. Ardle could barely contain himself. "That's it, Paddy. If that's spiv is going in there, there is where we need to be. You got that?" Paddy took his time to answer him. He was the slower of the two, a thinker who would take his time before risking all, unlike the excitable Ardle.

"No. Not with you at all, Ardle. I don't want to be going down the tunnel with a load of kiddies."

Ardle quickly pointed out that Ralph must know something that they didn't as he urged Paddy to follow him across the road to where the group had disappeared into the darkness. "Nope," said Paddy. "I'm still not with you."

"Sometimes, I wish you weren't Paddy. Now just follow me cos whatever he is showing them kids, we need to know about!" Ardle shouted at his Irish counterpart before striding back towards the entrance into the building they were standing in. Paddy crossed himself and jumped into line behind the quickly disappearing Ardle. Once out of the building, they both headed off across the road towards the small gap in the wall that Ralph and the children disappeared through some minutes earlier.

Paddy again crossed himself hoping to God that Ardle, "Knew what he was doing."

Once out of sight of the main street, Ralph and the children entered an eerie world, one straight out of the past, last seen decades ago. The walls were all neatly tiled in glossy cream and green similar to other stations in the area but were now all covered in dirt and grime built up over years of decay. Litter covered most of the floor area and the smell was horrendous, reminding the gang of the time they spent searching through the bins behind the slaughterhouse near the Smithfield market. The paint was fast peeling from the walls and ceilings of this dank place and what was once going to be a very grand station office, now looked like it had been used as a home for marauding flies who were all now dead and splattered over the glass and floor en masse.

Feeling their way along the wall in the darkness to the far side of the room Josey and the gang continually bumped and barged into each other and treading upon each other's feet much to their amusement. Suddenly, the gang realised that Ralph had disappeared and so the torchlight, by which they had been eagerly following him across the room. Slimey, the thinnest of the group, who had got his moniker because of his continual wet nose, was starting to have a bad feeling about coming into the building.

"Are you sure he came in 'ere with us?" he questioned.

"I saw him come in here," Josey assured him.

"Mister! Mister!" shouted Charlie Jr at the top of his voice. Suddenly, Ralph appeared and played the torch beam across his face which gave his features a grotesque appearance in the darkness, making the youngsters jump with fear.

"I can't leave you lot for five minutes without you making more noise than a heard of Heinkels. Now, if you want your nearest and dearest to know you're down 'ere, carry on," Ralph scolded them whilst chuckling to himself.

Slimey wiped another dewdrop from his nose onto his threadbare grey woollen top and was keen to know where he had disappeared to. The gang had, by now, all shuffled into the room as far as possible without quite standing on each other's boots and were now all standing against the far wall at the top of what appeared to be a huge spiralling staircase that descended into the depths of the capital.

"Look," said Ralph. "I was checking that the coast was clear so that we could go down into the tunnel. Now stick with me, tread carefully, and watch the rats."

Sniffing another belly full of dust encrusted snot loudly, Slimey eagerly replied, "I'm watching 'em."

But Ralph calmly explained that not everything he said should be taken quite so literally.

"No, I'm watching 'em, literally," Slimey told him, a nervous tone evident as he spoke.

Dismissing his comments with a chuckle, Ralph told the group to just, "Keep an eye out for them, that's all." However, unbeknown to Ralph or the others, Knock Knees had come across a huge rodent. A dark grey rat with the longest tail he had ever seen. Its eyes sparkling in the dim light that was still just creeping in from the early evening sky outside. He had silently and ever so gingerly placed it on Slimey's shoulder without him or any of the others knowing.

Again Slimey spoke, slowly, "But it ain't all, Ralph. I'm telling you." Upon hearing the concern in Slimey's voice, Ralph urged Slimey to explain himself. Letting out a huge blood-curdling scream that appeared to bring another two layers of paint off the walls, a terrified Slimey screamed at the top of his tiny voice, "Help me, Mister. I got one on me shoulder."

Ardle and Paddy had entered the room undetected by the others. Whilst all the commotion with Ralph's disappearance had been going, they both stood with their backs against the wall across the room from the others hidden by the darkness of the area they were in. Paddy was breathing deeply and balls of sweat were trickling down his elongated forehead, He took a large piece of dirty grey flannel from his trouser pocket and eagerly dabbed at his face trying to clear the sweat as it tumbled down his craggy face. They had both listened intently to Ralph and the children's conversation but something had irritated the luckless Irishman.

In a whisper, Paddy turned to his compatriot. "Ardle," he said.

"Help me! I think I got one on my head." But without even a nod in his direction, Ardle watched as the gang and Ralph started to descend into the tunnel area.

"No son," he said, "you just got nits, now will you get yourself together and keep up."

Having descended via an old concrete stairway, that was made up of about fifteen flights of steps with tiled walls similar to the entranceway with curved ceilings and old advertising posters still adorning the grubby walls, with much pushing, shoving and squeals of laughter, the gang of children and Ralph entered the disused station's platform. Immediately, the rush of cold air blowing through the tunnels underground network smacked them straight in the face sending a cold shiver down their spines. When they were all on the platform, Four Eyes searched out the unfortunate Slimey and immediately he berated him for screaming so loudly when they were all huddled in what was the old foyer room a few minutes earlier. Ralph quickly jumped to Slimey's defence, as he scolded Knock Knees in his jaunty way, for putting the rat on Slimey's shoulder in the first place, as he thought Slimey was about to have a heart attack, which prompted all of them to fall about laughing. The gang calmed down as Ralph brought some order.

"Right," he said, shining his torch along the platform, the

long trailing beam of white light hitting a myriad of orange boxes and wooden crates all stacked neatly off into the darkness of the platform as far as their eyes could see in the murky gloom of the old tunnel.

"This 'ere me good friends is the Victoria and Albert Museum," he said, as he strode purposefully along the old platform running his hands up and over all the boxes, shining a light occasionally into the box to reveal its contents

"You're 'aving a laugh, Mister!" exclaimed Charlie Jr.

"No I ain't, Charlie boy." As Ralph started to explain how everything had been bought down there for safekeeping at the start of Hitler's bombing campaign. They all began looking in the boxes, picking up the occasional work of art and trying to work out the correct way in which to view it. "Now, don't you nick nothing!" Ralph shouted as he saw Knock Knees place a small object in the pocket of his trousers. Knock Knees jumped back as Ralph put his large hand on the boy's shoulder. "Have a good look around. You'll never get this close to some of the countries most prized possessions again," he said as Knock Knees carefully placed the object back in its crate along with the other small gold items they had all been admiring.

As Ralph described to the assembled gang, the treasures that adorned the platform, Paddy and Ardle had crept slowly with the stealth of a hound stalking its prey, out of sight of Ralph and the children onto the old concourse and hid out of sight amongst some dirty old woollen blankets that had been thrown against the station wall after packing all the artefacts into the boxes, wrapping themselves into the blankets they remained out of sight of Josey, Ralph, and the gang.

An intrigued Knock Knees asked Ralph how he found out

about the tunnel and all the treasures that were on display. Charlie Jr who was climbing amongst the crates dismissed it all as a load of old rubbish, Ralph, however, was quick to point out that, "Although you may think its rubbish, it's actually as valuable as a hot dinner is to us," he said. Further, along the platform in the semi-darkness, Slimey, who was stood on what appeared to be another pile of old blankets left strewn across the old concrete station, moaned that he'd not had a hot dinner in ages, as he heard Ralph mention food.

Suddenly he shot back as he started digging into the old oil-stained pile.

"Blimey!" he shouted across to Ralph. "Look at all this!" Ralph rushed across to where Slimey was furiously tossing blankets in every direction. Ralph stopped and stared at what Slimey had uncovered, he barked a sudden command that bought them to a sudden standstill as they all stopped what they were doing and looked towards Ralph and Slimey further along the tunnel.

"Don't you lot touch nothing. I'll look at this lot, and that includes you, Slimey." Intimidated by Ralph's sudden change of character, Slimey panicked and dropped the blanket he had in his hands and charged towards where they all had come in disappearing out of view up the old concrete steps towards the surface. Ralph oblivious to his sudden change, just stood there staring at the mass of weapons and ammunition that Slimey had found, wringing his hands together.

Realism suddenly dawned on Ralph as he muttered quietly to himself, "My word, I could make a fortune with this lot." Josey edged himself closer to Ralph and without looking at the excited spiv, he gingerly enquired as to what was amongst the bundle of oil-stained blankets. "Guns!"

exclaimed Ralph.

"Loads of 'em!" Josey fixed a concerned stare on the huge cache of arms that Slimey had uncovered.

"Blimey Ralph! If we get caught in here with this lot we could get into serious trouble."

Still transfixed, Ralph muttered that as far as he knew, "Nobody saw any of them go in there."

"No, but they could have heard us," Four Eyes said. "Think of that screaming that Slimey did when that rat was on his shoulder." Josey thought about what Four Eyes had just said. "Look, Ralph, we don't want nothing to do with this lot. We don't need the aggro, do we lads?" he said urging the others.

"Look, no offence mate but I think it would be better if we all legged it. you can stay here if you want, but we're off, OK?"

Ralph was too engrossed to look up at the boy.

"Yeah mate, whatever you say. I didn't see you tonight. You didn't see me. You got that!" he spoke slowly making sure that Josey got the message. A quick nod from Josey sent the entire gang scattering for the exit, exploding in every direction as quickly and as noisily as they could, clattering up the staircase and disappearing into the darkness.

Ralph was now alone in the gloom of the disused station, or so he thought, as he continued to stare at his booty, he gave himself a moment before he spoke and slowly gathered himself. "What do I do with this lot then, do I do anything at all? Now, I know, I shouldn't, but what an investment this could be?"

Ralph allowed himself a wry smile as he considered his next move. "Christmas has come early in London this year!"

he thought.

He was still eagerly wringing his hands together when suddenly, away off to the right back down the platform by the entrance from where he was standing, there was an almighty scream. For a second, Ralph froze, not quite knowing what to do, he thought quickly to himself as the huge commotion carried on towards him. Boxes and all sorts were being kicked up into the air and crashing down with their contents spilling out onto the old platform. From this distance, Ralph couldn't quite make out what was happening but it was far too late to turn and run. Ralph braced himself for the unseen wave that was about to engulf him, when as quickly as it started, the noise and commotion ceased as the police officer brought the child under control. Four Eyes hadn't been quite so lucky as the others when running from the building and he had been cruelly snatched away from them and dragged back down into the gloom by PC Selby. Reenie's husband, Gerald, a solid hard-working Policeman of good standing within the local community.

PC Selby was a slight man who had just been tall enough to make the grade when he'd joined the Police. A copper's copper, he'd been on the beat for nigh on 15 years, always managing to get his man, although never quite earning the credibility amongst his peers for doing so, "maybe tonight?" was a thought that often occupied his mind and so some nights earlier in the week, when he'd spotted that the entrance to the old station had been tampered with. He made a decision that would see him checking it every night since whilst on this part of his beat to make sure nobody had been using it as a shelter or for anything illegal! He knew nothing of the treasures that had been stored in there, but whilst walking up The Strand earlier, he had seen from a distance Ardle and Paddy excitably disappearing through the boarded-up entrance at a rate that made them far too conspicuous for his liking and on prying back the sheet of corrugated iron that had been used to keep people out. He had nearly jumped out of his skin as Josey and the gang had all crashed past him in their haste to get away from what they had just seen down in the old tunnel. Four Eyes, however, had tripped on the top step of the last flight, twisting his ankle badly, making it difficult to move at the same swift pace as the others. He struggled in the gloom to keep his feet moving and get across to the opening out into the air, he crashed into PC Selby, just as the policeman had regained some sense of normality and his heart had stopped racing from the fright of all the children springing out on him. He clamped his muscular hands firmly around the boy's waist, Four Eyes kicked out and struggled like a wild animal but the policeman's grip was too good and he was unable to make it past the policeman and into the night air along with the others.

And now, here in the old station, the two of them were shouting and hollering at each other as the strong PC had dragged Four Eyes back down the stairs and onto the platform from where he'd run some minutes earlier to see for himself what all the fuss what was about. However, upon spying, Ralph stood a little way further down the platform staring into what seemed at first glance to be a pile of blankets covering something laying on the floor. PC Selby immediately thought the worst.

"Don't move, stay there and put your hands on top of your head." Ralph stood firm and said nothing as an eerie silence fell over the old underground platform.

"Is this your kid?" the policeman shouted. This knocked Ralph out of his gun-related coma, snapping him back into his usual more breezy self.

"Steady on mate. I'm not nicking nothing. I just stumbled on all this stuff," Ralph replied jauntily as he caught sight of Four Eyes, who was looking extremely nervous in the copper's grip. He felt sorry for the boy but his instinct told him that he needed to distance himself from him and any looming situation involving the guns. So deciding to take a slightly different tact, Ralph slowly started to explain that he was not in there 'nicking stuff' but looking for shelter from the bombings and that the "Kid was nothing to do with him." He eyed, a now tearful, Four Eyes but Ralph shook his head in his direction as he emphatically said, "No! He was nothing to do with him."

"No, he wouldn't be, would he?" said the policeman cynically. "Proper little Fagin you look like. Got all the kids running around, doing your dirty work then son." But still, Ralph tried to distance himself from the gang as he explained again that he was 'definitely' in there on his own and that the children had nothing to do with him, as he had just got in there when they all bundled past him at the bottom of the stairway leaving him stunned and just a little amused at their apparent hasty retreat. Again, the platform fell quiet as the trio eyed each other warily; the occasional sniffle from Four Eyes breaking the silence of the gloomy atmosphere. PC Selby took a deep breath and let out a loud audible sigh as he thought to himself that this was way too much of a coincidence.

Ralph knew that if there was one thing he had learnt in all his years as a spiv was to keep ahead of the game in difficult situations. He needed to keep on talking and fast but just as he was about to try and shore up his defence, Four Eyes decided to break the PC's vice-like grip on his grubby little collar. And with a swift movement of his skinny right leg, his tatty leather boot connected sharply with Gerald's left shin. The thud echoed loudly around the empty tunnels of the old Piccadilly line. Buckling under the immense pain, the policeman immediately let go of Four Eyes and fell to the floor clutching his throbbing shin and crying out loudly like a scalded cat. Breaking free, Four Eyes momentarily stopped and turned towards the stricken policeman.

"It's not true. He bought us down here!" he shouted, turning towards Ralph, who was standing with his mouth wide open aghast at the unfolding drama, his hands firmly clamped over his head, the young boy urged Ralph to help. "Didn't you?" He pleaded but Ralph remained silent, Four Eyes eyed both men quickly, in turn, searching for a response from either man that never came. Flicking them both a 'V' sign, he turned on his heels and sprinted down the platform towards the exit at the far end of the station faster than PC Selby could regain his composure.

"Feisty little bugger you got there!" he exclaimed sitting back and examining the scuff mark on his shin which was by now slowly starting to weep a small amount of blood onto his grey standard-issue police socks.

Ralph slumped his enormous shoulders and desperately tried to implore that the boy had nothing to do with him. Gerald sat there saying nothing, gently rubbing his aching shin. He grimaced as he touched the delicate skin that had been broken by the ragged leather of Four Eyes' tatty old leather boots.

"And while you're about it," Ralph said, rather

disdainfully, "how long have I got to stand here with my hands on my head?"

"I'm still thinking about it," sniped the PC. "Well, do you think you could hurry up? I'm getting pins and needles in my arms." PC Selby took a moment to think to himself when a dull thud was heard to echo down the platform off to the eastern end of the old station. Both men took stock of the noise and looked at each other.

"Probably rats," said Ralph. The policeman appeared to agree as he nodded silently towards the big cockney, again nothing was spoken; they eyed each other.

"This could be your lucky night, son!" said Gerald as he broke the silence.

Back amongst the gloom of the old disused tunnel where the two Irish men had been holed up spying on the unfolding events, Ardle grabbed the unfortunate Paddy as he tried to extricate himself from his miserable position and pushed him back down into their hiding place. His cramped legs would just have to ache. They couldn't risk being caught down there and any disturbance was sure to attract the attention of the policeman. Ardle glared at Paddy for causing the noise in the tunnel that had stopped both Ralph and the PC in the middle of their negotiating.

As they silently carried on spying on Ralph in his predicament, Paddy, still desperate to move some more to release his aching limbs, Ardle nearly exploded and in his rage, he started to emerge from their hideout as he heard the policeman tell Ralph it was his lucky night.

"Bloody hell Paddy! I think the coppers going to do a deal!" Paddy quickly grabbed the excited Ardle by his shoulder and pulled him swiftly back into their concealed vantage point. "What makes you think that?" Paddy asked more than just a little confused, Ardle said nothing as he just looked at Paddy and shook his head. His companion's obvious lack of intelligence was wearing him down. Quickly, they both settled back and tried to catch the rest of the conversation as Ralph and the policeman carried on their discussion further back down the platform.

Ralph looked at the copper dejectedly. "Oh yeah, I don't think so," he said, pausing a short while to take stock of his circumstances. Then, as his cockney charm and his survival instinct rushed to the fore, he dug even deeper to get himself out of the predicament he found himself in. "No, this could be yours; you got a wife at home?"

"That's none of your concern," the PC replied quickly, but Ralph carried on digging, explaining that he thought it may well be.

"She likes chocolate, doesn't she? Come on, they all do. What about eggs?" taunting Gerald as he went.

"You attempting to bribe me, son. I could have you up on a charge for that," replied the PC trying to get back a position of some authority but Ralph had now found his feet and was in full flow.

"No, no. Now that would be stupid, wouldn't it? No. Now look, you look, like you're not enjoying life at the moment, and I reckon that a little bit of good fortune on the home front may just improve industrial relations somewhat. Am I right?"

"Well," said PC Selby in an enquiring way, "I thought so," said Ralph. "Now, in my jacket pocket here, if you just let me take me hands off of me head for a little while, is something that will help, capiche." Excited, the old PC could hardly contain himself as he goaded Ralph to continue.

Ralph was now in control of the doomed PC, and he knew exactly what direction he wanted to steer him as he explained that 'he wasn't trying to bribe him' because what he was about to offer wasn't free. Especially as he didn't want him making accusations at a later date. Unperturbed, the poor old policeman quickly pointed out that he was 'no fool'.

Ralph looked at him; stood there in his badly fitting uniform, all covered in dust and grime from where he'd crawled through the gap to get into the station's old ticket office, a trickle of blood had found its way from the gash on his shin down over the top of his dusty boots, his custodian helmet sitting ever so slightly askew after being knocked awry when Four Eyes had kicked him, and for a moment, he began to feel just a tiny bit sorry for him.

But an icy blast from the tunnel jolted him out of his remorse and reminded him that he needed to get out of there as fast as he could without the wily PC charging him for being down in this part of the underground system without permission.

"I didn't say you were," he said, adding under his breath. "Well, not yet anyway." Ralph took a moment to weigh up his predicament again. "OK, let me look at you. Me thinks you're suffering from a lack of loving, am I right? No, no don't answer, trust me on this one. One bar of chocolate isn't going to cure this situation, two would help, but three. Now three and you just might start seeing an improvement. Now if you were able to add some bananas to this, I'm thinking you and the good lady might just see some fireworks. Am I right? Of course, I am." There was a long pause.

"You still with me?" Ralph added, for effect.

PC Selby had grown excited at the prospect of being able

to give his wife some chocolate or even some bananas as they hadn't been available for what seemed like ages, he almost burst with joy. However, he was still unsure of the unflappable Ralph and his motives, although, he thought, it did seem like the cockney spiv was offering him the keys to regain his wife's heart. "*Surely not,*" he thought to himself.

"This would be between you and me though?" he asked Ralph suspiciously. Quickly, a smile as wide as the disused tunnel spread across Ralph's face. Bingo! He had him where he wanted him. PC Selby then instructed Ralph to take his hands off his head.

Ralph relaxed his arms and shook them out down by his sides making more of it than was really needed. As he added a few sighs for good measure, clenching and unclenching his fists to get the circulation moving in his hands again Ralph looked up and started off from where he had last finished.

"I'm not going to ask you for a week's money, am I? That would be stupid, but you forget you saw me and the kid, yeah!" Pausing for even more effect, Ralph eyed a rueful Gerald, as he was nodding his seeming approval whilst gesturing Ralph to continue,

Ralph then delivered PC Selby his final proposal. They were to meet the following evening, out in his usual patch up on The Strand just by the entrance to the Aldwych station and whilst there, they could then agree on a payment for the PC turning a blind eye to seeing him and the children in a part of the underground system that was out of bounds to the general public. But there was one provision and the PC had to stick to it, he must take his wife, Reenie, along with him. Ralph had spied the PC and his wife, Reenie, strolling along, hand in hand, down Regent street earlier in the day whilst on his way to his patch and he'd thought to himself that she looked so beautiful with her long golden hair. He'd loved the fact that it wasn't tied back and curled up like the way the normal ladies had their hair, but she had it down, long and free-flowing. It glistened in the early evening light and there had been a slight breeze that evening and as it gently lifted her hair back, you could see her face to full effect, her translucent skin was totally unmarked and this showed off her features to great effect. They were soft and almost childlike and with the merest hint of rouge on her cheeks, Ralph was smitten. To him, she was the most beautiful girl he had ever seen, but he had noticed that there was an unease in the way she held his hand. Something wasn't right between the two of them and at that point, Ralph had thought that such a beautiful woman needed a real man to stroll hand in hand with, not a policeman with an ill-fitting uniform who couldn't give her the things that she needed. No, she needed a man or to put it plainly, she needed someone like Ralph, and, if, it was a big if, but if he could get close to her, he reasoned, that she may just be of a like mind and then he would be the one strolling down Regent Street with the beautiful lady on his arm. And then a while later, when he had been outside the station up on The Strand and Reenie and her two friends, Alby and Gertie, had threatened to 'lamp' him, when he offered his help. He had been taken aback by Reenie's pluck and courage and at that point, he knew she was the lady for him.

There was an eerie silence in the tube as PC Selby thought about Ralph's proposal for him to bring his wife along. He was puzzled and confused as to why Ralph would ask such a thing. Ralph could see that he had got Gerald's cogs whirring and so he stepped up the offer with one last teaser. He reached into the inside pocket of his grey flannel jacket.

Paddy, from his vantage point, further down the platform, suddenly grabbed Ardle in horror. "Bloody hell, Ardle! He's got a gun." But Ralph reaching deep inside the lining of his jacket took out a large bar of Cadbury milk chocolate, something that he guessed had not been on Gerald or Reenie's sideboard for more years than they cared to remember.

"Now," he said, "here's a bar of chocolate to be going on with." Pressing it firmly into the PC's grubby open hand.

"Oh, it's chocolate!" a somewhat relieved Paddy gasped as he spied the exchange taking place.

"Ah! He's a decent fella that he is," confirmed Ardle chuckling away to himself as they both stopped quivering from the fear of being a possible witness to the old PC's murder.

Gerald looked at the chocolate in a grateful manner. He was, of course, but he also couldn't help but think that Ralph still had an ulterior motive. "You know how to keep a man dangling," he said, pausing and taking a deep breath before he spoke again, "OK, tomorrow then."

At that point, Ralph knew he had him exactly where he wanted him and any way Gerald tried to turn, Ralph would be able to turn it back into his favour. Ralph turned towards the exit and with one last look at PC Selby, he stopped, holding out his hand for the PC to shake and quietly said, "I'm off then, OK, between me and you, yeah."

Gerald stood there impassively, seemingly refusing to shake the big man's hand. The lines on his furrowed brow growing deeper with every minute that ticked past. Ralph then turned away and walked towards the exit.

"Stupid rozzer," he muttered to himself as he walked

away not even caring if Gerald heard. He smiled to himself, but as he got further away from the policeman, he thought that maybe he'd said that a bit too loud. Not wanting to look back in case the PC had changed his mind, Ralph got to the bottom of the staircase. He took one final glance over his shoulder he was still alone the copper hadn't moved, he was in the clear, so lengthening his stride he took the stairs two at a time, gasping for breath as he reached the top. He thought to himself maybe the cigs should go after all, but as he stepped out onto the pavement, the night air was crisp and cool and a welcome comfort from the cold musty air that travelled around the dark underground system. Ralph straightened his trilby and smoothed down his grey flannel suit as he checked his appearance in the nearest shop window that was still intact and not too badly damaged from the blitzkrieg. He took out a packet of Capstan full strength, struck a match from the book he had in his back pocket and took a long drag on the crisp white roll of paper and tobacco. *Give up!* he thought to himself, *no that would never happen after all what harm can they do!*

Back down on the old platform, the luckless Gerald was still fixed to the spot. He still couldn't believe what he had just allowed to happen. Ralph was a notorious spiv, he was one who the police had been trying to pin something on for ages and he had just been his for the taking, but somehow he had managed to let him go and at the very least, all he had got for his troubles was a bar of flaming chocolate and for some reason, the one that he was struggling with, he had agreed to meet him again! And bring his wife along with him, that was the bit he couldn't fathom out at all. Reenie would love the bar of chocolate and she would love him because of it he thought and that 'was' a bonus considering the rows they had been having of late. But he also thought that Ralph needs to come up with a tempting offer otherwise he's let him get off scot-free. He could have earned himself a decent bit of credibility nicking that dirty little low life spiv.

"I'll show him!" he yelled at the top of his voice, up the Piccadilly line. Straightening up his uniform, he looked down at his grubby blood-encrusted boots, rubbing each toe cap in turn on his calves, he tried to get a bit of shine back into his appearance before he strode diligently towards the exit and out into the night air all the while cursing himself for his shortcomings.

After the PC had disappeared out of sight, Ardle was the first to emerge from the secret vantage point the two Irish men had established further down the platform. He checked that PC Selby had definitely gone and was not in earshot before he broke into an Irish jig as he rushed down the platform to where Ralph and the children had found the stash of guns. "Now this!" a very excited Ardle cheered, "This is what will make the trip worthwhile!"

Paddy had also extricated himself from their underground hiding place but was some way behind Ardle, picking his way around all the piled-up crates of museum artefacts. Breaking his silence, "What seeing the fella con the copper!" he yelled after the joyous Ardle.

"No!" Ardle fired back. "You fool, all these bloody guns." Paddy arrived at the spot where the guns had lay hidden.

Standing stock-still, he paused, breathing silently to himself as he had thought hard about what lay in front of him. This knocked the momentum out of Ardle's celebrations.

Quietly Paddy spoke, "But you heard the fella." He said,

"He's already laid claim to them."

Ardle's eyes deepened as he scratched his stubbly chin, the dark and grey whiskers belying his real age. He tipped his Khaki green woollen flat cap back, so the brim rested high up on his forehead showing his rapidly receding hairline in the gloomy tunnel light. Chewing the inside of his left-hand cheek, he gave Paddy's last words a lot of thought.

"Well," he said, "perhaps we need to have a word with fella before he speaks to the police!"

Simultaneously, they both turned in silence and began to trudge along the platform towards the old exit sign, stopping occasionally to rifle through the boxes and crates that had been stored there. As they reached the exit and the first step up and out into the London night air, they turned around and looked back along the station to check that they were still the last people there and that no one else had been around to witness what they had both seen. Quickly, they then hurried back up the spiralling stairway towards the fresher night air, desperate to leave the stench of old London behind them the further they rose up from the depths of the tube system.

Paddy stopped by one of the many old variety bills that lined the staircase and as he was about to comment on one of the acts, a particularly large rodent slowly but surely scampered its way up the handrail stopping every so often to stand on its rear legs to briskly clean its whiskers off after feeding further back down the stairwell. As it moved along the rail, its long tail swished from one side and then to the other as it closed in on Paddy who was totally unaware of its impending presence. It scampered past the Irish man, its tail catching his nose as he leant forward and peered closely at the poster. Letting out an almighty scream, he fell back down five steps, landing in a pile of old newspapers and rotting rubbish that had been blown around the passageways over its years of closure. Further up the stairs, Ardle, who had by now reached the next landing area, curled up laughing at the stricken Paddy who was trying to get to his feet amongst all the rubbish. Rubbing his sore back and brushing his trousers clean, he picked up his woollen hat and suddenly without hesitation, flew forward taking the steps two or three at a time. He ran past Ardle in fear of the rat showing itself again and then burst out of the old station foyer out into the night without looking back or stopping to check whether Ardle had managed to get himself together.

At the corner of Drury Lane and the Aldwych, Paddy stopped, he placed his hands on his knees and gulped down huge amounts of air, as he looked back to where he'd just come from. Ardle was slowly making his way along the street, still delirious with laughter after Paddy's brush with the foul rodent. Eventually, Ardle caught up with Paddy who by now had caught his breath and was pulling on one of Irelands finest Carroll's Number 1 cigarettes. Coughing and spluttering, he put his arm around Ardle and they both collapsed in a heap, laughing to themselves about the evening's activities.

***

As Charlie sat on his upturned orange crate, he couldn't care that a splinter from the sharp wooden box had pierced his leg in the fleshy part at the back of his thigh. His ears were throbbing and the sharp pain from the crack to his head was far more significant. He checked his trousers, they were in a mess from where the blood had dripped from the huge gash he sustained just above his right ear. The Red Cross auxiliaries who were stationed there at The Aldwych station had dressed the wound and Charlie now had a neat, if rather flamboyant, bandage encircling his head and some sticking plaster on the other cuts he suffered whilst he'd proudly sat on the makeshift toilet which had been sideswiped from the powerful blast near to where it was situated upon The Strand and now tending to his wounds with great care and enthusiasm, as they sat further along the platform from the others was Connie who had taken a shine to Charlie earlier in the evening as they had tried to entertain the platform full of people, but now as she wiped away the rest of the grime and dust, Charlie shook his head and moaned ever so slightly.

"Cor my 'ead is killing me," he said. "Who'd a thought Hitler would get you whilst you're minding your own 'aving a good old fashioned tom tit."

Raising an eyebrow at Charlie's rather coarse cockney dialect, Connie dismissed his injuries and urged Charlie to pull himself together. Whilst she continued to tenderly wipe away his battle scars and he continued to moan about his lot. Connie reminded him that it should be easy for him, after all, he wasn't bad for an old one.

Charlie's ear pricked, he wasn't old at all. Well, he didn't think so. Alright, he'd lost a fair amount of his hair, but he blamed that on his mum's side and the wrinkles were probably due to a lifetime of Winnie's nagging.

Although Charlie was quick to point out her error, Connie just couldn't understand why he was with them in the tunnels if he wasn't that old? Why hadn't he joined up? Why wasn't he away fighting the war? Charlie's natural instinct to be the joker passed the conversation off with a quip and he told

Connie that he could tell her why he wasn't away fighting but then he'd have to kill her. Charlie chuckled away to himself as he felt that his joke had been extremely witty; Connie, however, just raised her eyebrows again and carried on cleaning his face and as she gazed into his deep blue eyes still surrounded by the small flecks of dirt picked up from the blast, a sudden thought crossed her mind: *he was so good looking if he wasn't old, he must have been running away from something.* So she asked him outright. Again, Charlie carried on his witty charade as he told Connie that he wasn't running away from anything as he had flat feet.

Connie felt just ever so slightly prickled as Charlie continued joking around.

"Don't you ever stop joking?" she said in a sharp waspish tongue.

Suddenly, realising that on this occasion, he may have met his match, Charlie took a deep breath and slumped forward on his orange crate, as he composed himself. He appeared to wipe some more grit away from around his swollen eyes as if this was to blame for the tears that had started to well in large pools in the bags that were gathering beneath his war-weary eyes from all the sleepless nights in the underground.

"Look, Connie, it's all this," he muttered whilst pointing mutedly up and down the platform, clearly upset. Connie could clearly see the dejection in Charlie's face and his voice was portraying a man in deep turmoil with his surroundings, but her enquiring mind needed to hear more from him.

"All what?" she enquired of Charlie probing deeper.

Not ready for his reply, it shocked her nonetheless, she could tell it was coming from a younger man, a much younger man than she thought as quietly Charlie explained that it was the bombing! The war! And that he didn't agree with it. That we were all losing our families and our possessions even our friends, but most of all we were losing our dignity.

"For a better world?" he asked, although he spoke gently, she could feel the anger in his voice.

In his hushed tone, he spoke softly as he asked Connie what she thought, whether she really believed that all the death and destruction would lead to them being happier? Connie was perturbed by Charlie's thoughts, but on seeing her reaction to his comments, he changed his tack.

"Look at you," he said his voice rising as if in defence of his thoughts.

"I'm not in your class, I don't pretend that I should be, but because of this war, you've lost your dignity and you're having to spend time in this hellhole just so you can be safe." Charlie had, by now, risen from where he was sat and was pacing the station platform. His disgust at the situation they found themselves in was plainly visible to all who took notice. Every now and again, he kicked at a piece of rubbish that had been dropped on blown along the platform by the trains or their passengers as they had passed through earlier in the evening. Connie rose and marched up to where Charlie was now standing, pushing him back down hard onto another orange box, she loomed above him trying to generate as much superiority as her tiny frame would allow.

"I've not lost my dignity!" she roared, but as she did so, up and down the platform their companions for the night, all suddenly looked up from what they were doing and glanced in their direction. It dawned on Connie that it would be best if she kept a more dignified approach, pausing momentarily as if catching her breath before she spoke again, this time in a more calm and respected manner she carried on, "It's the way you cope in situations like this that determine whether your dignified or not, not whether you were born with a silver spoon in your mouth."

Charlie quickly realised he'd taken on more than his usual cockney wisecracker and given the reality of the situation, it would best if he kept quiet. Connie hadn't finished, she continued to berate Charlie in a more quiet tone so as to keep the argument to themselves. She told him about how she'd seen him help people out when they'd been stuck on the station or on the stairs, over the last few nights that she'd been there and how she'd also seen him helping the elderly and the youngsters when they'd needed a bit of extra special care because they had been frightened or lost.

"That's where your dignity comes from Charlie!" she exclaimed. Charlie couldn't get a word in at all, no matter how hard he tried, Connie would not let him interrupt. She carried on, telling him that there could be "No dignity in any of our consciences if we objected to fighting for peace because the more prepared we are to stop this onslaught together, the more we can work together."

Charlie pondered her last statement as she stopped to regain her composure before another round of her well-meaning dialogue was skilfully aimed at Charlie's weakest point.

"So you think you're a conscientious objector?" she said as she prodded Charlie in his chest, his now heavy head firmly resting in the palms of his hands, too weak and embarrassed to look Connie in the eye. "But that's not you, not the real you."

Connie then softened as she urged him to think about the

consequences of being locked up for being a conscientious objector especially as he had so much goodness inside of him. Eventually, she finished her long speech by telling Charlie that whilst he was still young, he should stand up and be counted and that he should be "flaming well dignified about it."

There was a moment's quiet as Charlie slowly raised his heavy head from the palms of his mighty hands and looked peacefully at the beautiful young face in front of him. In that brief moment, Connie saw a man who believed in what she had said. Charlie's huge palms that had been creased with a thousand manual jobs, now slowly came to rest on Connie's small and bony shoulders. She, in turn, brushed aside her hair and swiftly tucked it back behind her ear as it had fallen from its neatly coiffured arrangement. For a moment, they gazed into each other's eyes, Charlie and Connie were oblivious to everything around them as they became immersed in their awareness of each other's beauty. Connie made the first move, as she tilted her head towards Charlie, her deeply painted red lips locking with his, they embraced each other oblivious of their surroundings. Without a thought for their own companions somewhere else on the platform, at that moment, nothing else mattered; certainly not the war!

Charlie was the first to break this unusual connection, he was a million miles from her world of butlers, servants, and bone china tea sets. "Blimey Con, what's all that about? You're a bit upfront, 'ent, you girl?" he said blaming Connie for their unexpected tenderness.

Charlie was completely knocked back by Connie's witty reply, as she told him that he was so good looking, how was she supposed to keep her hands to herself. "And you say I'm a joker." Charlie rather uncomfortably was quick to point out.

Suddenly, out of the corner of his eye, he spotted Winnie stirring from her slumber further back down the platform. Instantly worried about what she would say about his apparent closeness to the beautiful socialite, he sat up and distanced himself from Connie, pushing the crate and himself backwards which created an annoying scraping sound that echoed around the tunnel. Connie, taken aback, looked at Charlie to find out the reason for his sudden retreat, but his eyes were like those of a rabbit's caught in her driver's carriage lights she thought, as Charlie added a slight nod of his head back towards where Winnie was, still prone but already barking out her commands to those in her immediate area.

Connie sensing that Winnie would be more than a bit displeased at what they had done, appealed to Charlie not to say anything as, she added, "That wives don't tend to see it for what it is." Still guessing, Connie's kiss was not all it seemed, Charlie sternly looked Connie in the eye and demanded of her whether it was, real, or was she 'just taking the mick!' Begging Charlie, Connie pleaded that she wasn't 'taking the mick' as he thought, but that didn't mean that he should go telling his wife about their lustful encounter.

"Wife!" Charlie exclaimed laughing. "You've got no worries there girl, Winnie's me sister, well, like me sister. We grew up together, same blinkin' street, we seem to have lived together since then, even when she got married, I lived at her house." This news appeared to settle the apprehensive socialite and Connie's interest in the handsome man in front of her seemed to blossom more. She decided to enquire more into his relationship with the ever-domineering Winnie, who by now, was pacing her space on the platform like a caged zoo animal enquiring as to Charlie's whereabouts and berating those who kept quiet and said nothing. Charlie kept his head down low so he couldn't be seen or heard by her, hopefully, he willed, the other people on the platform would keep quiet too.

"So where's her husband now?" she whispered to Charlie, her interest growing more as each second passed.

Keeping low, he too answered Connie in hushed tones, "I don't know, in the army somewhere fighting." She nodded, pleased that Charlie was not romantically attached to his companion. But Charlie felt he needed to share more and began to tell Connie about losing his family when he was young. His parents had contracted typhoid from contaminated food and Winnie's family had taken him in straight away, without a thought for themselves. Never telling the authorities what they had done and he reasoned that this was why nobody knew where he was and why they probably hadn't caught up with him to enlist. She sat back on her slim legs as she kneeled before him, his worn ruddy features beginning to turn sad as he remembered his youth back in the east end with its poverty and overcrowding. Charlie continued telling Connie what he thought she should know, "Beneath all this bravura, I'm a mild man I find it hard to understand why we are fighting each other. I may, well, fight, I'll probably have to. But it needs to be when I'm ready, do you understand?" Connie gave this some thought before she answered in her usual forthright way as she told him that although she understood what he was saying, she couldn't condone his actions.

"Maybe, I could help instead of fight. Look, I don't have any skills that others could use," he offered.

"Of course, you do," said Connie enthusiastically, as she reminded him that he was fit and healthy and that time was on his side. Connie paused for a short while before adding that it might also depend on how long he had actually been running? Charlie's chin dropped, he took offence at Connie's last statement, he hadn't been running at all, and he told her in no uncertain terms, "They've never actually caught up with me."

"OK," Connie said slowly, not sure of how or what she was going to reply with. Usually, she was very quick to put others of her own social status in their place. She could have a harsh tongue if needed and this coupled with her fine grasp of the English language, she could stand her ground or make her point felt amongst some of the country's most eminent orators. But she was definitely struggling with the jaunty East ender in front of her, and so decided that she should use some of her own school girl wit to put him in his place, and with an ironic smile on her face, Connie told him in her best, concerned but mischievous tone, "Just because they haven't caught up with you doesn't mean that you couldn't volunteer your services. No one is going to be stood waiting for you with a big stick to thrash you with."

A huge smile began to rise within her, suddenly exploding into roguish chuckles as she playfully added, "Maybe a big lacrosse stick. Charlie, what do you look like in shorts?"

Connie's sudden change in tack was complete, coupled with her extraordinary reference to an outdoor pursuit that was more suited to her peers, running around during game breaks several years earlier. The look on poor Charlie's boat was a picture, confusion reigned, not for the first time was the errant cockney being put in his place by the beautiful young girl who was sharing this little corner of the station platform.

But still unable to see that she was fast becoming smitten on him, he challenged her in a more aggressive tone. "What are you on about?"

Connie thought long and hard about her answer before she coolly dismissed it as her, "Mind just wandering around a bit?"

Charlie hadn't worked out that Connie was trying to be flirtatious. Still being assertive, he urged Connie to get back to the matter they had originally been discussing. She paused and looked deeper into Charlie's eyes, her pulse started to quicken further as her need to be desired by this rough diamond sored and looking to the nearest member of the public on the platform, she passed her thoughts on. "Wow! A bit of rough who's domineering too!" The young lady sitting to the left of Connie, on an old crate covered in a ragged woollen blanket, smiled back at Connie nervously, not wishing to become involved in their discussion.

Connie however, now felt she had an ally in the young lady sitting to her left and as she continued to question Charlie, "Are all cockneys mean and moody?" She would every now and again nod or gesture towards the young girl as if she was part of the debate.

Charlie's face creased ever so slightly at her last comment and grinning he asked Connie politely if she'd 'been on the sauce!'

Connie smiled at the realisation that she was slowly winning Charlie over and decided that now was the time to be slightly more blunt in her quest to win Charlie's heart. Jabbing a decidedly bony index finger deep into his cavernous chest, "You're not getting the hint!" she told him determinedly, his eyes suddenly came alive. *Hallelujah!* Thought Connie.

Suddenly, a light shone brightly within Charlie's head and as his grin turned into a more seductive smile, he slowly realised that Connie wanted more than a helping hand with her suitcase each night. Connie continued to dig into what made Charlie tick as she asked him what he was good at, whether he was "Good with his hands!"

"There you go again," Charlie snapped dryly,

"For pity's sake Charlie!" she replied sharply trying to appear less naughty. "Are you good at anything, I mean what's your speciality?"

Pausing for just a brief moment as if to capture Connie's full attention, Charlie with an unbelievably wry smile spreading contagiously across his stubbled chin, added amusingly that he's "really good with his hands!" before almost falling from his comfortable perch on the disused orange crate as he lolled from side to side completely immersed in his own humour.

Connie gave him time to regain his composure and to wallow in his own amusement for a short while before reminding him that he needed to get himself cleaned up and that they needed to find someone to talk to about his future. Charlie took umbrage at her comments about his cleanliness and slowly took a handkerchief from his waistcoat pocket and attempted to vigorously wipe any more grime from his face. Chuckling though, Connie reminded Charlie that he was after all just a little bit smelly.

"I don't know Connie, I smell a rat." Charlie observed still not completely sure of her motives at all.

"Hmmm," Connie mused quickly before reminding him that he did just have a toilet and its contents explode over his head. Dissolving into a sniggering heap and giggling like two love-struck teenagers, Charlie and Connie quickly but quietly stole themselves down along the platform area towards the exit, past a small group of children, many of whom were by now soundly sleeping on their made-up beds. Ducking under some temporary clotheslines which had been strung up between several rusty old bunk beds, the lines all containing tonight's washing, smelly old damp vests and shirts and so on, their owners trying desperately to get it all to dry so that it could be pressed in time for another busy day's work in and around the capitals business districts. Slowing to negotiate their way around a pile of old woollen blankets that a scruffy dog of disputable parentage had made a home for the night, Charlie and Connie neared to where Winnie was half sitting half lying on a bed made up of a trio of old wooden tea chests that had been pushed together and covered in some of the blankets from the pile. They stopped dead still and paused a while, making sure that she wasn't looking in their direction, she wasn't, she was totally engrossed in a game of crib that was going on between two older ladies with an old splintered playing board and match sticks for pegs. The cards had seen better days and looked marked in favour of the owner as the two ladies started to argue over the rules, Winnie lent over and offered her knowledge of Cribbage telling them she had been playing the game since childhood completely forgetting that the two old girls had probably been playing a lot longer than her, making their combined knowledge of the game more suitable to winning the small argument over the score. As Winnie became more and more engrossed, Charlie and Connie slipped past and made for the exit. As they reached the bottom of the steps, they lengthened their strides and took them two at a time until they reached the fresher air out on

The Strand. As their feet hit the pavement, Charlie immediately stopped and impatiently looked around him as if searching for something or someone.

"What are you doing?" Connie asked Charlie inquisitively. She was almost breathless from their sprint up the spiral staircase, giddy with the excitement of knowing she was alone with Charlie and unsure what their next move was to be. They had escaped from the depths of the capital into the cool night air of a London under siege from Hitler's bombers. Whatever they did, they had to stay safe.

"Looking," Charlie quickly offered as if this would justify for an answer for the odd way in which he'd ground to a halt as soon as he was out in the London nights air.

"For what?" a confused Connie asked again.

Charlie had his serious face on again. "I'm looking for someone in authority." Connie laughed.

"Charlie," she said, he noticed that Connie had a glint in her eyes and for one minute, one totally unexplained minute, it reminded him of when they won the Sunday meat raffle at the Crown and Dolphin in Cannon Street. Something he remembered, Winnie, her husband and him doing before Winnie's husband went off to war. It fed them for nearly two whole weeks, there wasn't a scrap of food not used and their bellies were swollen after dinner for hours.

"Charlie!" Connie snapped him out of his daydream. "We have a whole evening. War isn't ending anytime soon." Connie knew a small flat nearby, just off Drury Lane as she stayed there when she had appeared at the Theatre Royal. The owners of the flat were never there as they lived in luxury on the Cote d'Azur and besides, she'd only spoken to them once when she first needed somewhere to stay. And as far as she could remember, they'd said to her anytime she was in town she could use it. A key was supposed to be always resting in a little nook where the plaster had cracked over an alcove at the bottom of the entrance passage in the hallway at number sixty-six. If no one was staying there, it would definitely be there, she hoped and they could go and use it and as most were out sheltering in the tube system, they would definitely have at least a couple of hours before being seen near the building by anybody other than the odd stray cat wandering aimlessly around looking for some scraps or some rancid mouse to feed on. They snuck swiftly into Drury Lane. It was quiet, save for the sound of bombs detonating way off in the distance over Tilbury way. Hitler was giving them some punishment tonight as if they hadn't had enough already, the lights in the street were out in accordance with blackout regulations and it took Connie a short while to get her bearings.

"Quick over here," she whispered in a hushed tone to Charlie who was following the young socialite close behind like a small puppy. She had found the small alleyway in which the flat was off and once they were both in the alley and out of sight, Connie pushed the big old wooden door at number sixty-six. It creaked in a melodically strange way as if it was screaming tunefully on its rusty hinges as it swung inwards to reveal an extremely grand and ornate hallway that looked as if it had recently had a visit from the decorators, the smell of newly painted distemper hung heavy in the air. "Oh blast!" Connie exclaimed, forgetting for a moment that she should be quiet and talk only in a whisper. "It looks like it's all been decorated since I was last here," she said, lowering her voice until it was barely audible to Charlie and *rather nice too* thought Charlie. After years of living in a crowded two up two down near the dockyards, Winnie's place hadn't seen a lick of paint since the day it was first built back in the previous century. So to see a freshly painted room and to breath in its newness was a delight to Charlie's senses.

Connie moved immediately towards the alcove which was on the back wall straight in front of them as they entered the doorway about fifteen feet away. She felt around in the dark, her eyes still needing to adjust to the new surroundings until she managed to locate the bottom of the small alcove which was about three feet up the wall above the ornate skirting that surrounded the room, praying the decorators hadn't filled in the crack she felt around. Immediately, her luck was in, the key was just resting on the ledge, the decorators must have just put it there after repairing all the cracked plaster. Grabbing the key and Charlie's hand, in turn, she headed blindly for the stairs to the first floor with Charlie scampering along behind her. Months of entering the building at the dead of night after performing at The Theatre Royal meant Connie could walk around the building from memory.

After a long walk up what was obviously a grand staircase that swept to the left as it rose, Connie and Charlie came to a big yellow door with a large polished brass letter 'C' screwed to the door at eye level. After putting the key into her right hand, with her left hand, she moved the decorative escutcheon plate to one side and slid the key into the hole as she had done many times before. Her hands trembling almost violently as she did so, she'd never bought a male companion back with her. Besides, she had always sort permission before bringing anyone back to the flat. As she turned the large rusty old key, a loud clunk was heard as the levers inside moved up and down before finally resting in the open position. Connie pushed the door and said a quiet, "Hello" as she did so, just in case someone was in the room. She paused for a brief moment before going into the flat, her senses were going into overdrive. She needed to be sure no one else was in the flat before going any further.

The smell of fresh paint was evident in the flat as well, Connie went over to the large picture window on the far wall directly opposite the entrance door and closed the big heavy cotton and gold silk curtains before walking back across the room to the big round switch on the wall by the entrance door. Flicking the arm in a downwards motion, the huge glass chandelier that hung magnificently in the centre of the room lit up. All the while, Charlie had stood stock still fearing any additional movement or sound could bring people running from all corners of the building. But right now, Charlie blinked uncontrollably for a few seconds as his eyes accustomed to the bright light that had exploded into all its glory in front of them both. Looking around, Charlie took in all the majesty and splendour before him.

"Bloomin hell, Con! I didn't know this kind of stuff existed." She smiled back at him, amused by his simple tastes as she closed the big entrance door behind them and guided Charlie swiftly towards the splendour of the bedroom. Tonight was going to be something he would remember for a long time. The officials, on the other hand, could wait just a little while longer.

***

Hitler's bombers had been coming in over the docks at Tilbury and hitting their targets for at least half an hour now.

80

The skies were a leaden grey and the air full of the smell of explosive material as the great searchlights swung back and forth through the night sky dragging huge arcs of white light across the sky in search of the machines bringing death and destruction to the streets below them. Alby, Gertie and Reenie had been settled into the large but equally uncomfortable Anderson shelter at the bottom of Reenie's back garden for at least two hours. And the tall white candles that Alby had managed to secrete from the rear of the church over at Spitalfields the week before last, had burned a significant amount of the way down. Although the cross was still evident even if Alby had tried to scratch them out of the candles so no one would know where they came from. The night air was cold for the time of year and the rusty old sheets of iron which had been roughly placed in the garden to look like a small tin shed and then covered in soil to form a bank up and over the small building did nothing to keep the chill of the outside where it belonged. All three of them were lying on some dirty old blankets which were being kept off the ground by some old wood Alby had scavenged from one of the bombed-out houses further down the road a couple of days earlier and turned into a badly laid jigsaw puzzle on the dirt floor.

Earlier in the day, Reenie had managed to reclothe Alby in a suit from the wardrobe of her late Uncle George. Alby had chosen a lovely dark blue double-breasted one from George's neat collection. It had been cut to perfection, almost as if it had been tailored for Alby himself. Uncle George had last worn it on the day before he died and Reenie insisted that Alby kept it in perfect condition. He, in turn, assured her that his intention was to make sure that he returned the suit to her as soon as he could in perfect condition. Reenie trusted Alby but as far as returning the suit unmarked, she knew better than it coming back in perfect nick.

Alby, like the others, was freezing cold and he'd drunk a lot of Reenie's tea throughout the day and after two hours in the shelter, the only thought on his mind was that he needed to go to the toilet and when he needed it, he needed it now. The two ladies were getting his backlash.

"I can't help it," he said. "Look, do you reckon I could make it to the lav before we get the next round of bombs," Alby asked again after his previous rounds of pleas had continually fallen on deaf ears,

Reenie nodded her head trying to urge Alby along. "Give it a go," she said to him. "But," turning to Gertie, she added bluntly, "he better not pee himself because Uncle George would never forgive him if he relieved himself in his Sunday best."

Desperate, Alby reminded her that George wouldn't know as he'd been, "Pushing up the daisies in the family plot for the last five years."

Reenie replied tersely, she was not happy at all. "I'm not washing trousers that you've peed yourself in. You had plenty of time to go before we came in here."

Alby argued that before they all got in the shelter, he, "Didn't need to go, I couldn't have gone if I'd tried."

For five long minutes, they sat in total silence even the bombers seemed to have taken a break. Gertie was the first to break the cold damp tranquillity. "We should have gone down the tube," she said. Quick as a flash, Reenie countered that that was Alby's fault as well.

"Why?" Alby asked, upset at this latest round of finger-pointing.

"Made yourself look like a fool in front of that spiv, didn't you," she answered almost smugly.

"I bleedin' didn't," Alby said.

"You bleedin' did, Alby," she countered. "You should have lamped the spiv when you had the chance."

Alby was not having this. He told them both that he'd have looked a right heathen stood there fighting in his underpants. He still had his dignity despite losing all his clothes in the bombing and besides, he would have ended up being handcuffed to her Gerald.

Reenie grumbled sarcastically that didn't they all look "blooming dignified sat at the bottom of the garden under a bit of scrap iron." Alby reminded her that half the country was doing exactly the same.

They sat in silence after this latest outburst for a number of minutes before Reenie, eyeing Alby, sat across the shelter from her squirming in pain due to his need to pee. Very quickly, deciding they needed some humour to lighten the evening's uncertainties, slowly and melodically, Reenie started to speak but almost to herself, "Drip, drip, drip, drip." She smiled, giving Alby, whose hands were by now firmly pressed between his legs, a jovial nod and a wink.

"Leave it out, Reen," Alby retorted. He sounded desperately short of breath as he tried to concentrate on not wanting the toilet.

"Drip, drip, drip, drip, went the April showers," she continued.

"Reenie! Blooming hell woman." Alby was in a state, desperate for the toilet and Reenie's joking was not helping the poor man

"Come on Alby I'm only having a laugh," she assured

him, but Alby was not in the mood, and he told her so.

"Bloomin' funny ain't it," he said in a rather terse manner. Gertie who had been silent through most of this exchange couldn't resist one last twist of the knife and told Alby that men have 'weak bladders'. Reenie keenly added that men were 'weak, full stop'. Gertie felt that this was a bit strong and told her so.

Reenie had had enough, sitting in the cold waiting for the all-clear had given her pins and needles in her legs and Alby's constant moaning was giving her a headache. She was not finished and she thought to herself that Alby was set fair for more of her verbal attacks.

"No, it's not!" she said. "Look at him!" Shoving a neatly manicured finger out towards the hapless Alby and catching him in the ribs on his right ticklish side. For a moment, Alby squirmed and chuckled to himself, forgetting about his desperate predicament.

"Two cups of tea and the poor old bugger's breaking his neck. Does he chance it and go in his trousers? We could be in here for the night, or does he chance it and leg it up the garden, dodging the tin bath and the washing line and find the karsey in the dark before (a) a bomb gets him or (b) next doors dog thinks he's a looter and bites him on the arse." Lifting herself from her uncomfortable bedding and looking Alby straight in the eye, she continued. "Either way," she said, by now getting extremely agitated, "he ought blooming well hurry up and make his mind up about what he's going to do, then we can all get a bit of shut-eye!" As she finished this latest condemnation of Alby's handling of his situation, she flopped down on her makeshift bed turning her back on Alby and pulling her spare blanket high up over her cold face.

Alby paused for a moment before making a bold statement. "That's it," he said, "I'm going!"

"Oh, Alby not in them trousers." Gertie was aghast, she thought he meant he was going there and then right where he sat, and a night spent in the flimsily built shelter with no running services after he had relieved himself was not something the slightly built east ender had wished for.

Alby grovelingly assured her he hadn't but was merely stating that he was going to chance it out of there, out in the open air of the back garden as he hadn't heard a bomb explode or one of Hitler's bombers for a while. Reenie who was still miffed from their earlier altercation spoke in a muffled tone deep from under her covers, "Might get the all clear then!" she said.

Gertie urged Alby to go and get it over with. "I'll time you," she said nonchalantly,

"I'm not some blinkin' athlete," countered the beleaguered Alby.

Reenie goaded him some more from under the covers, "You're all talk Alby. Say one thing and do another." Alby quickly thought about what she had just said and then quickly rose to his feet as best he could in the shelter's tiny space, adjusted his jacket and making sure he did all the buttons up he looked around the shelter for one last piece of much-needed equipment.

"Who's got the torch?" he questioned the girls looking at them both in turn, this bought an amused chuckle from under Reenie's covers. Alby stood there, staring inquisitively at the body shape underneath the blankets where he'd last seen Reenie disappear a few arguments ago.

"You can't use a torch, can you!" exclaimed Gertie.

Finally, Alby was quick to remember the blackout rules and shook his head in a disgruntled manner.

"Bleedin hell!" he swore to himself as he cocked his ear to the side of the shelter listening for any sounds that might delay his departure. "Can you hear that dog?" he asked, sure he'd heard a noise and whilst searching for agreement from both women in the shelter, a resounding 'no' came from Reenie's direction whilst Gertie who was made of a gentler compassionate nature offered a more subtle 'no'.

Alby was sure he'd heard something, scratching perhaps. "That's the rats, bigguns and all," Reenie offered with a sarcastic twist that getting bitten by one of the rats might be nastier than getting bitten by a dog. Reenie then enquired after Gertie's thoughts on the matter, quickly picking up on her sarcasm, Gertie continued the theme, telling Alby that they were big with extra-long teeth that liked a bit of 'soft flesh'. "Pop your head out and have a look." Reenie urged Alby. Nervously, Alby lent out of the open end of the rusting shell.

"I can't see anything," he said.

"What? No dog or nothing?" Gertie replied from deep within.

Alby, his head sticking out of the shelter as far as he could physically get it, was feeling the chill of the cold night's air suddenly rushing down the gap between his collar and the exposed neckline of his shirt. Quickly, he decided that it was all or nothing and as he told the girls again that he couldn't see anything because it was too dark he was just going to have to chance it. Alby suddenly made a dash and disappeared out into the darkness of the cold night's air, just at that precise moment a large dog, (Alsatian, maybe?) was heard howling off in the distance.

"Blimey that was quick," Gertie sniggered. "He must having been bursting." Unconvinced, Reenie sat up and reminded her that it was she who had told him that he was 'weak' and with that, she then rolled over once again and tried to get a bit more comfortable in her improvised bed.

"But didn't you hear that dog?" Gertie asked.

Reenie just rolled around a bit trying to get comfortable and told her that "He'd be alright."

Outside, Alby had fought his way up the garden tripping occasionally on the broken clay flowerpots that Gertie had discarded around the borders after a good summer's crop of begonias and hyacinths that she grew from scratch. He knew if he'd trodden on any of her prized blooms, he would be in trouble but desperate times called for desperate measures and he'd answer to her later for any crimes committed against horticulture whilst scrabbling around in the dark. It was a long garden with borders running along both sides and a small fence made up of two long wires separated Reenie's from next door's garden and in the summer, Reenie had made it a beautiful haven with gorgeous displays of flowers of every colour and size masking the richly dug soil. And if he wasn't mistaken, somewhere she had started to dig a pond and try as he might try to avoid falling into it, he knew falling in would leave Reenie shouting the odds for getting the suit all covered in soil and grass. So, treading carefully, he strode on towards his destination. As he reached the tiny outside toilet, he lifted the rusty catch on the old wooden door that was still in need of a good paint after another dry summer where Reenie had promised to give it a once over. And he squeezed into the small cold smelly room, catching a moment, he stood there in the darkness trying to retune his senses to the environment, listening out for any strange noises. Alby started to pay his call to mother nature. He started to whistle, as was the norm, usually to make people aware the toilet was occupied but this, he also did out of habit rather than a nervous disposition and he was getting louder with every tuneful note.

Gertie turned to Reenie, chuckling to herself after hearing Alby, whistling away to himself, stood alone in the dark. "Stupid fool. Who's going to use the bog?"

"It must just be a habit." Reenie chuckled as well. Back in the small outside karsey, Alby finished his call of nature and yanked firmly on the chain causing a huge flush of cold water to splash into the china pan below. Reenie let out a huge sigh upon hearing this and took it as a signal that they would, at last, be able to get some kipping done. She closed her eyes, shifted around for a few seconds to find a comfortable spot on the cold wooden floor and attempted to recall her thoughts from earlier in the day to help her get to sleep.

Alby adjusted his clothing and backed out of the tiny space, closed the door making sure the catch was firmly shut, he turned and started to make his way back towards the shelter. His memory was working in overdrive to find his way back towards the shelter without tripping or falling over in the dark. As he stumbled blindly towards the halfway point between the shelter and the toilet, suddenly, from out of the darkness a massive snarling, angry dog struck, in an instant hitting Alby, hard from behind sinking its teeth firmly into his flabby buttocks chewing and gnawing at his flesh. Alby screamed and yelled at the top of his voice as the dog dragged Alby to the ground in a mass of flailing arms and ear-splitting howls from both the dog and Alby. Desperately trying to get the dog to withdraw and leave him alone, Alby kicked out as best he could at the dog.

The attack was savage and severe; Uncle George's suit didn't fare well and burst open across the whole of the backside revealing Alby's torn flesh. Crying out in pain, he screamed for help, Reenie screamed at Gertie that the bloody dog had got him, but between them, they were unmoved, too scared to venture out in case one of them became the dogs next victim. Alby was mumbling as the pain hit home, screaming that he should have, "Just peed in the trousers in the first place." The dog released its grip on Alby's buttocks but immediately took up residence at the bottom of his legs pulling at the turn-ups at the base of the trouser legs trying to drag Alby back into the darkness from where it had come. Desperately, Alby clawed at the ground, trying to find something to grab and hold tight to stop the dog from getting any more purchases. The tops of his fingers became sore and blistered as he did so but still, the dog pulled Alby along the rough ground for some ten feet or more before Alby was able to free his belt and kick the remains of the trousers off. The dog sensed the sudden release but instead of making another lunge at Alby, it suddenly turned and ran off in the direction it had attacked Alby from.

Alby lay there shaking as the shock of the brutal attack set in, clutching at his mutilated wounds, the pain etched across his ageing face.

Far above in the night sky, a lone Heinkel bomber had arrived over London far later than all the others, who had, by now, finished wreaking their own havoc on London some half-hour earlier. Having been lost whilst flying over the channel due to a navigation error, the Luftwaffe pilot headed for the beacons of light, the fires, caused by the earlier evening's Blitz of London, threw up into the night sky and so when he finally arrived in the general area, he should have been a lot earlier in the evening, he released his deadly payload as quickly as he could before turning sharply back into the direction from whence, he'd come.

Quietly, the bombs fell through the sky like a hail of black rain; slowly at first, before gathering momentum as they fell towards earth to wreak havoc on the unfortunate city below. Gradually, the bombs started hitting their targets that had been directly under the line of flight the German bomber had taken. At first, starting further across the dockyards to the east of the capital, before they started to creep closer towards where Gertie's house was, throwing up devastation and catastrophe on each impact. The final bomb neared its intended target and poor old Alby was still writhing on the ground in agony blissfully unaware of what was racing towards him from the night sky.

It struck, a few yards from him, throwing dirt, concrete, and Gertie's famous prize-winning gladioli skywards as it buried itself into her back garden. Miraculously, the bomb stayed intact, failing to detonate. It smoked and hissed as it cooled down in the chill of the September sky. Alby frozen, still by the shock, looked up at the huge mass of twisted steel yards from his feet as Reenie popped her head out from inside the shelter. "Flaming hell, Gertie! That was close!" she shouted at her stunned friend, totally unaware of Alby's predicament. "Gertie there's a hole in the garden!" she cried to her stunned friend quickly coming to her senses. Gertie, too, popped her head out of the shelter. She cried out for Alby at the top of her voice, but the garden remained silent. Reenie looked at her mate and with a quivering hand, pointed towards the garden.

She spoke slowly, measured, making sure Gertie understood what she had to say, "He better not have ruined those trousers."

***

The Aldwych station platform was, by now, almost in total darkness, save for the odd beeswax candle its tiny flame dancing in the gloom of the Piccadilly line creating giant silhouettes on all the walls that the tiny light could reach as the last of the travelling Londoners slowly but surely wound their way around all those sheltering on the platform.

The last train had passed through the station sometime before and as old Elsie looked at her tiny pocket watch, she declared it safe to descend onto the tracks so that the children could tie their tiny hammocks to the lines and get some sleep.

"Come along children. It's way past your bedtime, the last train ran half an hour since; now give me a hand to tie these sheets onto the rails." Elsie had by now climbed from the platform onto the track below. Her frail old body creaked as she did so and now as she passed out the crisp white sheets, she'd spent the day laundering, to all the small children, she urged them to get busy and make their makeshift beds for the night.

Josey and most of the gang had all met back up at the station after their impromptu tour of the tunnels by Ralph earlier that evening and were all keeping quiet about where they'd been and what they'd been doing that night. It was, after all, time for bed now and they could talk about it tomorrow when the oldies were all out of earshot. Josey, as the leader, had already decided that they should have another look but that next time they should go alone, keeping Ralph out of the picture. It seemed a sensible thing to do as they'd heard he was a wrong un, always operating just outside the law and it just wasn't worth getting into any strife with their parents just to keep Ralph happy. Four Eyes had been caught but as he'd got away without having to give his name to the stupid copper, another shot was worth it as the old bill wouldn't be looking for them in particular. And as long as they all kept their eyes peeled, when they went down through the old entrance and into the old lobby area and nobody saw them, it was worth having a go. None of them was interested in the guns that Ralph had already declared were his, they were looking for things that they could fence around town to make a bob or two to help them through the war and to put some food in their tiny bellies, some chocolate would be nice.

Josey was half-sitting, half-leaning against the back wall of the tube station reading an old copy of the Beano he'd found discarded in the entrance lobby when he was coming back in. And as he chuckled, sometimes hysterically, at the escapades of Lord Snooty and Biffo the Bear, he would look over the top of the comic and eye the situation in front of him. Right now, he'd caught sight of the children, all desperately trying to tie a knot in the sheets that Elsie had given them. Kate was the first to speak, as she caught his attention, Josey quickly dropped his head as if he was intently reading his comic.

"Come on, Josey. Get them all together, the quicker the better."

Josey was a big lad for his age and the fact he'd even shaved the occasional hair from his pointed chin, there was no way that he was going to be associated with the smaller, younger children, so passing her request off, he shouted over, "I don't sleep in those things, I've found me own bed, over 'ere!" Josey had always been the leader of the pack though, long before the war had bought everybody into the tubes and the gang had got bigger, so Kate tried a different tack.

"Some of the little ones need your help, your guidance Josey. This is hard on them, we aren't having much fun." Josey took a deep breath and let out a big cheerful sigh, rolling his newly found copy of the beano up and shoving hard into his back pocket so it didn't fall out, he stood up and looked up and down the station at all the forlorn faces of the younger children kneeling between the rail lines trying to tie their bedsheets between the rails to form a snug, cosy hammock. Josey scratched his chin as he gave Kate's request some thought.

"OK," he said. "I'll help out but you ain't getting me sleeping in those hammocks again, not like last time." Adding, for a touch of humour, "There's blinkin rats running up and down them rails." Josey chuckled to himself as he thought his joke was hilarious.

Kate, however, was furious at Josey's last comment and told him so. "Things are bad enough at the moment, so there's no need to make things worse with stupid jokes." Josey cringed to himself, embarrassed that his joke had tripped him up.

A little girl's voice, further down the rails, broke the atmosphere caused by Josey's joking. "I can't tie a very good knot, Josey," the little girl said, trying furiously to tie a knot to make her bed between the cold iron rails. "If I wriggle when I'm asleep, I'm sure it'll come undone." She looked at him desperately, in the hope that he would jump down and help her tie the sheet on. "Give us a hand, Josey," she begged him.

Josey could sense all eyes were on him to do something about the little girl's plight and whilst he suddenly enjoyed the attention everyone was giving him, he too felt uneasy about getting it right and so gingerly, he made his way towards the youngster shivering in the cold air between the rail tracks.

"'Ere give it 'ere," he said nonchalantly as he climbed down to the rail track and reached the young girl. "We don't want you falling out in the middle of the night." Furiously and competently, Josey started tying the first knot and with a big friendly smile and a playful wink, Josey finished the task. The little girl then took over, straightened it all out and then jumped in. Making herself comfortable, she gave Josey a huge smile, her dirty face framed by little ringlets of golden hair cascading down her face. Josey was a proud boy and so as he looked up from where he had just tied the young girl's bed sheet to the rails, he asked all the other children if anyone else was having trouble. Quick as a flash, every little child's hand up and down the Piccadilly line shot up; straining their little arms, they pointed them as high as they could towards the ceiling. "Alright, one at a time!" Overwhelmed, Josey shouted at them all. One at a time, he moved down the line, tying each sheet safely onto the cold cast iron lines, making sure he did his best to not get any grease from the rails on his hands or the sheets that he was tying and then, in turn, making sure that all the young children were tucked in comfortably. When he got to the end, he stood up and took a long slow bow. He was almost revelling in his status as number one amongst all the children.

94

Raising his arms to get their attention, he then placed a single finger across his lips, indicating he needed them to be quiet as he addressed them all, "Now kids, I can't sleep with you tonight. I'm too big, but I'll be over there all right, sleep tight." And taking one final bow, Josey snuck off towards the tunnel wall, took his crumpled beano out of his pocket and quickly got back to Lord Snooty and all his chums.

Elsie, dressed in an old blue floral dress with a scraggy hair net tightly pulled over her greying hair, all neatly styled in rollers for the next day, moved forward to take charge again as she did most of the nights they had been down there having once been matron at a boarding school in Sunningdale, she still knew how to get the youngsters to behave themselves properly at night time, whilst their parents sometimes just let them run around upsetting the older members of the community every night until Elsie arrived and took charge.

"Come along now, children. Let's get our heads down and close our eyes." She had an immediate soporific effect on them as all the paper aeroplanes they had been throwing at each other stopped and the card games amongst the older ones stopped abruptly too.

Jenny, a tiny petite little girl, who had always placed herself in the middle of all the children, had slept uneasily most nights. She always appeared at the station alone along with her little knitted night bag which contained her hairbrush and a small, wetted flannel that smelt of rose petals. At around six years of age, she was always a sweet and charming young lady who never gave any of the adults' cause for concern and she had never spoken unless she was spoken to. Suddenly, she stood up as Elsie moved along the line of children, some of whom were already snoring loudly after a day of playing in and around or on the heaps of rubble left behind after the weeks of bombing. "I say, lady, you're pretty," said the young girl as Elsie neared her.

Elsie was used to all manner of children calling out in the dead of night after her many years working in Sunningdale at the boarding school and so as she moved towards Jenny, she herself said, "Thank you very much," in her deep aged cockney tongue as she then proceeded to tell Jenny that whilst she too was also very pretty, she urged her to go to sleep.

She waited by Jenny's makeshift bed for a moment before moving slowly along the line, quietly singing an old English lullaby as she passed each child. In turn, she patted each of their tiny heads and muttered a small prayer for them all, for God to get them safely through the night. Just as she reached the far end, Jenny, who had still been restless since Elsie asked her to go to sleep started crying, gently at first, her sobs slowly gathering pace until she was weeping uncontrollably. The other children started to wake around her and Elsie urged them to be quiet and to go back to sleep. Quickly, Elsie moved towards where Jenny lay weeping into her knitted night bag.

"What's the matter, luvvy?" Elsie had heard many replies to someone's fitful sleep over the years but Jenny's response to her question came from as far afield as she could imagine.

"I've just seen my daddy here, and he kissed me goodnight."

Elsie thought for a while about her reply, before she sympathetically told Jenny that she shouldn't cry, as her daddy wouldn't want that. Through her tears, Jenny carried on though, "But how did he come here? Granny said he had died fighting."

Elsie quietly asked the little girl where her mother was, as more of the station's community that night started to become aware of the little girl's plight, they had all taken pity on the child as she's seemed a lonely young scrap walking to the same space each night and always alone.

Jenny sat up and composing herself in a very assured and mature way, she told Elsie that she didn't know where her mother was, but that daddy had said she was with him! "But that can't be right…can it?" She asked, curiously.

Looking around the many concerned people on the station platform for some kind of assistance, any assistance, Elsie asked Jenny if her granny knew where her mummy was? Jenny slowly looked down into her tiny, knitted bag and pulled out a small envelope containing some very old looking dog eared pictures of two people in what looked like a pose from a wedding. As she looked at the pictures, slowly, she brought them to her tiny lips and kissed each one in turn before solemnly looking at Elsie and the many faces on the platform all looking on, she spoke in a slow but very deliberate voice, "I think my mummy is dead, but no one will tell me though. "

Pausing briefly Elsie asked the little girl, "Where's your granny tonight?"

Jenny's reply was quick and very matter of fact, "At home, I think?" Pausing for a while before she added that her grandmother had told her to be safe and come down the tube.

Jenny's bonny little face had become ashen as she relived some obvious horrors in the recent moments of her tiny life. Starting to tremble Jenny's voice took on a more worrying tone, "Please, will you look after me, I'm scared. I'm scared that granny won't be there in the morning just like mummy."

Elsie moved closer to Jenny and wiped a small tear as it

dripped from the corner of the small girl's eye onto her pale dirt-encrusted cheek. Elsie cradled her into her large bosom and assured Jenny that they would look after her.

At that point, Jenny looked vulnerable, afraid, and alone.

"Close your eyes, my darling," Elsie spoke quietly to the bereft child. As Jenny slowly started to drift into another restless sleep Elsie looked up and down the line at all her new charges and speaking slowly and softly in a dignified whisper matching her caring manner, she told everyone,

"In these times, it's hard to feel safe, and the brutality of this situation is probably lost on all your young souls. But our lives are changing, and the hurt may continue for some time." On hearing her mellowing voice, the myriad of faces on the platform slowly started to stop what they were doing as they looked on, many with pools of tears slowly starting to well in their grimy eyes.

"Our sons, our daughters, brothers, sisters and our mothers and fathers will all do what they can to help. Peace, I am sure, will eventually be among us. But until that time, we must gain the strength we need through our God and our thoughts." She paused as if she was in deep thought, connecting with her inner spirituality as she caressed the small gold cross that hung around her neck. Turning back to Jenny, whose eyes were tightly shut as she softly breathed in and out, she teased the little girl's hair to one side.

"You say your daddy came to you. Well, he probably came to show that he still loves you and believes in you." A small smile started to appear on Jenny's face as the little girl stirred.

"He and your mother may have gone from your life, but the strength they had is now your strength, use it. They cared for you and ultimately gave their lives for you." Jenny's eyes remained tightly shut but she was awake and listening intently to what the old lady had to say.

"Don't cry, my darling, be strong. Our mothers and fathers are always with us wherever they or we may be." Elsie slowly rose from where she had perched next to Jenny and sat herself down on the platform edge, mindful of the grime that ran along the face of the old brickwork that had formed the platform all those years before.

As she sat there smiling down at the little girl, Jenny opened her eyes and in her most confident voice, she spoke to Elsie, "Daddy said he was happy now and that mummy was too. I'll always treasure his last kiss, it was right here on my cheek, I can still feel it, and then daddy was gone. If mummy and daddy are happy, then I must try and be strong. I want to sleep now. Goodnight, lady."

"Goodnight, my dear," Elsie then began to once an again pass amongst the children singing her old lullaby, confident that she had put the young child's mind to rest, as every now and again, a small sob was heard among the adults who had all stopped and listened to what Elsie had said.

The night was icy cold in the tunnels and the winds that blew along with them added an extra chill. The children slept soundly that night and never moved despite the small visitors that crept up and down the tracks looking for any small scraps that had been dropped into the sunken lines. Elsie had kept her promise and had moved her belongings down onto the tracks so she could be close to Jenny, so the young girl felt safe. And Josey? He'd spent the night going over the previous day's events and what he and the gang were going to do with all the treasures that Ralph had shown them. He'd read his

Beano from cover to cover and back again, just in case he missed anything the first time around and it was now discarded on the station floor along with screwed up copies of yesterday's Mirror and The Times which had all been read thoroughly by those sleeping rough in the tubes and also those that had struggled to get any sleep at all in the poor conditions so far underground.

Up and down the entire platform, along with those snoring loudly or talking gibberish in their sleep, were those that were playing cards, crib, or any other games that they had brought in to amuse themselves. It was bitterly cold, and most had wrapped themselves in old woollen blankets and pulled their hats firmly down over their ears to keep warm and shut out the annoying noises that many created during their sleep.

As the night wore on, those that were playing games slowly put them down to one side and drifted off into a safer place and dreamt of the good times they had before Hitler had declared war on Europe. The bombing had stopped hours ago and slowly as night turned into the early morning and the sun started to rise over the bomb-ravaged sites of the east end, London started to go about its usual daily business. The workers had woken from where they had spent their night and dressed in their best bowler hats and suits with umbrellas, just in case, and the ladies slipped into their heels and placed their fancy hats upon their perfectly styled hair; ready for another day in the office or butchers or market places.

As the first of these started to arrive at the stations around the network of tubes that served London's business district, the station masters proudly displayed their uniforms as they greeted them all with a good morning and they hoped that everyone they greeted yesterday had woken safe and well and that Hitler hadn't paid them a visit the night before. The trains began to pull out from their overnight berths and started to trundle into the labyrinth of underground passageways to arrive promptly at their designated pickups around the network.

Victor had been awake since five a.m. and in the time since he awoke, he had thoroughly cleaned his boots with a heavy black wax till they shone in the morning mist that surrounded him as he stood out in his cold back yard. His freshly pressed uniform hung neatly behind the kitchen door, out of the way of the lard that sizzled in the pan, eagerly awaiting two eggs that were resting on the side waiting for his wife to turn them into his breakfast feast. Victor too had a friend in Ralph.

An hour later, he was clean, dressed and his stomach felt like it was fit to burst after such a monumental breakfast. It was mornings like this he remembered why he'd married the good lady. Her cooking was certainly high on the agenda, but right now, he was pedalling furiously west towards central London to make sure that all was as it should be on his arrival at the station. Victor, who had proudly looked after The Aldwych and had done so for more years than he cared to mention, arrived in good time. He put his bike safely in his office and then slowly prepared the station for another day. Starting with the ticket office, he made sure it was functioning properly and that the young lads who he thought *couldn't be trusted* selling the morning papers, hadn't encroached too much into the lobby. He swept the main entrance and slowly moved his way down into the depths of the station where a few of those who had been sheltering the night before still happily slept, blissfully unaware of the time and that the trains were about to come trundling through the station as they do on any normal day. Victor strode onto the platform with an air of dignified authority, his chest thrust forward, strutting, to show who was boss during the day.

Most, if not all the people, had already packed away their belongings. All the children had already awoken and moved from their beds suspended between the rails and there was now only a handful of people still huddling in their makeshift home; Peggy was one of these. She'd drunk far too much the previous evening and was still sleeping heavily in a drunken stupor as Victor came up alongside her. Gently, using the tip of his very shiny thick leather boot, he gave her a small nudge to her left shoulder hoping that would be enough to wake her. She didn't stir and so Victor once again prodded her, a bit more sharply this time and whilst Peggy let out a small sigh she still didn't wake up from her slumber. Victor had to get her up and moving quickly before he was able to complete all his station checks and so with a swifter prod with his boot, this time in her left buttock, and a heavy shake of her shoulder. Finally, he then bent over her and got as close as he dare, the smell of her breath was choking.

"Come on now, Peggy; up you get." He coughed at the stench of stale alcohol and cigarette smoke that wafted from Peggy. He carried on loudly in his best station official's voice, "The trains start running soon, time to get this station back to normal."

Peggy suddenly sprang to life and after she'd taken a good look around look around through ghastly eyes at the few stragglers that were by now moving wearily along the platform, she let her early morning frustrations get the better and in a loud voice, slurred by the previous night's alcohol that still hung heavy within her system she started to rant at Victor, "Clear off you old busy body. What's wrong with you people, always shoving us about. I was running things around here when someone was still wiping your nose."

Victor found this amusing, but mindful of the fact he still needed Peggy to get up and move without causing too many problems. He spoke to her in a softer, kinder, caring tone, "Of course you were, Peggy, and there's nothing wrong with having your memories, but for now shake a leg and move on."

Peggy stared blankly at Victor, paused and with a critical look, she slowly started to rock back and forth.

Her eyes belying her alert state, still deep in her drunken stupor, she started to see red and at the top of her voice, making sure all that were still present could hear her outrage, she decided to vent her anger on the hapless station master, "Put 'em in uniform and they all end up like that, thinking they can run before they can walk." Peggy was almost screaming at the top of her voice.

Everyone, by now, had stopped what they were doing and were watching eagerly as Victor was trying but failing miserably to control Peggy. She became more and more animated, swinging her arms wildly around she gesticulated to all and sundry.

"Why should we all go back up top? We'll only get blown to bits. No, it's not safe, I tell you. It's not safe, we can't go up there. The blooming bombers are coming back; help us for God's sake, help us," screamed Peggy at the top of her now incensed voice as she ran from person to person, her eyes now wild with fear. Victor grappled with Peggy, desperately trying to control both the situation and her, but Victor was no match for Peggy when she was in full flight.

"Blooming hell, Peggy! Get a grip, will you, love? Here, someone give us a hand!" yelled the desperate station master, begging those around him to come to his rescue.

Around them, there were those who had stayed to watch Peggy lose her grip on reality started, slowly they came forward to reassure her. Ethel more quickly started to push her way through the melee to reach the stricken Peggy. The two women had been best of friends for many years, each looking out for the other when times had been hard, and Peggy needed her comforting hand and reassurance now!

"Here, come on, love. It ain't going to do you any favours getting all upset. He'll only get the rozzers on you." Peggy's mood changed dramatically as soon as Ethel started to talk to her in her soft east end brogue, "Cheer up the sun is shining top side I've already been and had a look."

Taking an old well-worn silk handkerchief from its home tucked high in her cardigans sleeve, she dried the tears that had started to flow over Peggy's grime-stained cheeks. And taking her arm firmly, clutching it to her body, comforting her like a mother would comfort a distraught child, she turned and looked at the crowd of people. "Right, everyone stand back. Me and Peggy are leaving now, give us a bit of breathing space."

Taking a deep breath she turned back to Peggy and with a final wipe of the precious silk hanky that she had been given by an ardent admirer many years before when her looks were worth more than they were now. Time had not been on her side, it had marched ferociously through her pockmarked face, she said: "They won't recognise you when we come back; we'll have you looking like a new penny."

Quickly she whisked Peggy off before another word was

spoken, to sober her up and give her a good clean before either of them would need to make the evening pilgrimage back down into the tunnels again later that evening.

Victor and the others stood there silently for a few seconds reliving what had just occurred over and over in their minds, Slowly he gained his composure, removing his station masters cap he ran his fingers through the greying mop of hair that he'd flattened earlier with a good dollop of Brylcreem, pushing each greased strand of hair back in place before replacing his cap in his impeccable manner and then he started to usher those still left on the platform to hurriedly go about their way and to clear some space for the travelling workers who would soon start to besiege the tunnels as they went about their daily business. Victor clasped his hands behind his back proudly pushed his chest out and with a swagger, he strode off towards the far end of the platform moving discarded blankets and boxes to the side as he went. In the distant tunnels the first trains of the day could be heard winding their way through the passages before stopping at their designated stations, London down here at least was getting back to normal.

***

It had been another glorious September day in the capital, the birds had sung all day and much of the debris from the previous night's bombings had been cleared to make it easier for people to travel around the main thoroughfares. The Strand had seen its share of luck again over the last few nights and remained relatively untouched. In the area of Aldwych station, the businesses that lined The Strand were all now beginning to close their shutters and bring in the goods they had displayed in the streets for eager Londoner's to buy, the news stalls were now all starting to display the evening newspapers and young newsboys were cheerily whistling their way through another shift of selling papers.

Peggy and Ethel were stood on the steps of the Adelphi Theatre sheltering from the glare of the late evening sunlight as it moved speedily across the capital before finally setting way over to the west the likelihood of the bombers returning was high and they would be starting off to the east in the dock area as it got dark. The theatre was much further down The Strand from the station where Peggy had caused such commotion earlier that day but this was also more generally the area in which they would both often ply their chosen trades, but tonight they were both making sure that their make-up was still perfectly intact, not smudged and that they had dressed in their very finest clothes to show everyone that even those who had questionable jobs or who were just, questionable, could still stand shoulder to shoulder with the great and the good of the capital and behave in a way that would be a credit to them. Peggy was still feeling dreadful about her display on the platform earlier that day and had told all those who would listen throughout the day that she "I isn't going down the tube tonight".

Ethel stood back and admired the person stood in front of her. "Never let 'em get you down that's my motto," she told Peggy adjusting her collar, so it didn't look out of place and mindful of Peggy's insistence that she was not "going down the tube."

Ethel asked her once more, "'ere where you sleeping tonight?"

Peggy knew she had nowhere else to go, a night in their tiny flat with bombs dropping all around them wouldn't be at all comfortable and so resigned to her fate she admitted to Ethel that of course, she would have to once again go down into the underground system, unless, she added, "Ralphie got summat better."

"Ralph?" Ethel said trying not to be too sarcastic. "You and Ralph got something going then?" she knew that there was absolutely no way the cockney spiv working The Strand would in any way be interested in her wayward friend.

Peggy stood there smitten, a look of love plastered all over her face as she spied Ralph casually sauntering along The Strand in their direction, his odd gait was distinctive in that part of town you could spot him a mile off, everybody knew when he had stock on him and when he didn't, even the police who patrolled that area knew, but Ralph was becoming too ingenious, too cunning to be caught that easily and as she eyed him from afar, she turned to Ethel, almost dribbling, at the sight of her unfortunate target.

"Lovely 'en he," she said clearly smitten with the charismatic Londoner.

"You've lost your marbles Peg." Ethel laughed. "Ralph wouldn't want the likes of us, he's far too busy chasing money."

As Ralph neared to where the ladies were standing, he stopped briefly on seeing them there and immediately, he turned his back on the pair checking his pockets and the lining of his jacket making sure his evenings stock was still where it should be and that there were no authorities lurking to disturb his activities as he tried to blend himself into the busy background.

"Go on then, Peg," urged Ethel "There's your man, go and see if he's got a bed for you for the night."

"He's working. I can't just go and butt in," said Peggy.

"He's not working, he's on his own!" Ethel snapped,

"He's working. That's why he's ignoring us." Peggy was having none of it.

Ethel rolled her eyes skywards as she mocked Peggy. "He's ignoring us 'cos he don't like us."

Peggy paused for a moment as she considered Ethel's last comment the tone in her voice sounding hurt at Ethel's last observation, "He's not ignoring us 'cos of that."

Ethel, however, continued to have a dig at Peggy, "No! Go on then Peggy what gem could you possibly come up with to convince me that Ralph 'ent ignoring us."

"'Err, he's on special OP's and he can't be seen to mix with the hoy paloy." This, she thought, would stop Ethel's continued baiting of her fondness for Ralph,

Ethel looked at Peggy, incredulously at first and then she looked back at the tall man stood yards from them in his long black coat and Trilby his dark shoes gleaming in the evening light, she was sure what Peggy had just said about Ralph was a total load of nonsense, but she still needed to ask Peggy who it was had told her about Ralphs special role,

Peggy responded that she had heard it somewhere in passing, and that was good enough, she didn't need confirmation from the man himself.

Ethel decided to put the old bag lady out of her misery, she couldn't let her continue down this route and so she told Peggy that what she had really heard was that Ralph was on the 'police special observations notice' which meant he was likely to be nicked shortly, especially if he put one foot out of place again, so there really wasn't any possibility of him, taking a chance, in being seen with the likes of either of them.

It was hard but Peggy needed telling, Ethel felt awful as she watched Peggy's face crumble the more she took in what Ethel had said but with one further last twist of the knife Ethel called over to the cocky spiv, "Oi, Ralph! Tell Peggy here that she don't stand a blooming chance with you."

Peggy looked on at Ralph pleading him to give her one more chance but as he slowly and deliberately looked her up and down her smile balanced precariously her eyes begging Ralph to show his approval of her, Ralph quickly brought her back to earth with a bump as he barked sharply back, "Clear off will you, both of you, I got work to do."

Peggy's lips immediately began to tremble, slowly at first but quickly becoming a mess of spontaneously quivering jelly, as her tears quickly appeared and started to descend from the corners of each bloodshot eye.

"Told you!" Ethel whispered in Peggy's ear sarcastically.

Walking along The Strand, towards The Adelphi in the full glare of the evening's sunlight but across the road from where Ethel, Peggy and Ralph were stood arguing, was Reenie and her husband, Gerald the Policeman, the very man who had the previous night caught Ralph 'bang to rights' in the old disused station, and now unwittingly she was about to arrive at the appointment Ralph and Gerald had arranged between them.

Reenie had spied Ralph from way back down the street as they walked towards the theatre and her neck had bristled as she remembered her meeting with him at the Aldwych station with Alby and Gertie previously, they closed on where Ralph was standing gesticulating wildly at the hapless Ethel and Peggy. Gerald seemed amused at the odd trio's altercation and pointed them all out to Renee as trouble with a capital 'T'.

"Alby nearly lamped him yesterday, he was pulling all sorts out of his jacket."

Reenie loved being able to tell her husband about the many villains who crossed her path although Gerald was not always impressed as Reenie was never very discreet and tended to tell him when they were in public, making it look like 'he' told his wife everything about his job.

"Will you shut up?" Gerald said to his wife. "It's him we've come to see. Now go and tap him up."

"What!" Reenie exclaimed. "What do you mean tap him up, what kind of girl do you take me for, you stupid idiot."

Gerald was well practised in giving Reenie short shrift and she generally did as Gerald told her and so it was not going to be any different on this occasion as Gerald quickly explained that 'he' couldn't be seen 'fraternising with him', he pulled Reenie closer into him so no one could possibly hear what he was about to tell his beautiful young wife.

"What's wrong with everybody?" Gerald hissed. "We all want a little bit more than we're getting but nobody will do anything for it," he spat spitefully in her ear.

"But you never said we was seeing some bloomin' spiv," Reenie replied quietly, it never went in. Gerald was stood there, half taking in what she was saying, but the other half of his thoughts, the more dangerous side, were on Ralph across from them and whether he was going to try to set him up again, he hadn't forgotten the last time they'd met and how he, 'Ralph, the dirty little low life spiv', had conned his way out of the tunnel.

However, a thought suddenly crossed Reenie's mind as she looked across The Strand to where Ralph was, standing with his back to Ethel and Peggy, she remembered that Ralph was a 'good looking boy' and 'that if she used her noddle a bit thing might start to look up'.

"Hmmm," she mused to herself. After her initial thoughts about the meeting with Ralph, Reenie was no longer backing away, she adjusted her dress and scarf and preened herself in readiness for her big moment.

"Alright," she said calmly to Gerald. "You go and stand over there." Wagging her finger in the direction of a shop doorway across from where they had stopped just as Gerald caught up with what Reenie was saying.

She started again in her inimitable way adding arrogantly, "Move them stupid women along or something," as she pointed at Ethel and Peggy, "And get out of sight; I'll do the hard work."

Gerald raised his eyebrow and chewed his bottom lip whilst giving Reenie's comment some thought, pausing for a short while he eventually nodded in agreement and moved slowly off across the busy street towards where the smitten Peggy and Ethel were stood, they were in no mood for what Gerald was about to say. As he closed in on them he raised his arms towards them in a way that told them, that in no uncertain terms, they were to start walking, in the opposite direction and as quickly as possible, this was his patch and it was not going to be a place for working girls, Gerald didn't want them starting in this part of London, this was a fine salubrious area where families walked to the theatre of an evening, Gerald was not knowingly having prostitution on his beat.

Peggy was the first of the two girls to say anything as Gerald approached sternly, "What do you want?"

Gerald continued gesturing to the two of them to move along as he slowly approached in a stern but calm manner, Peggy looked at Ethel as she continued, loudly in her distinct caterwaul, "Blooming Nora stand here for five minutes and the blinkin rozzers come out of every nook and cranny."

Gerald, had now stopped and was standing right beside the ladies on the pavement on the north side of The Strand as he offered the girls what he considered was a rather witty reply, "It's who you're stood with Peggy. You should know better than to stand with Ethel, you know, when you're out on the street."

"Oh, that's nice!" Ethel was clearly upset by what the Policeman had just said adding, "My reputation follows me around then."

"No," he said sternly, with a rather wicked twinkle in his eye, "It's the smell Ethel," as he wafted his hand back and forth in front of his nose, looking at her almost mockingly. "Now come on, no aggro, move along."

Ethel had been moved along on many occasions before, but this was different how dare he tell her she smelt she always made sure 'she' was clean at the very least even if her clothes left a lot to be desired. Ethel shot Gerald a look that told him he was in deep water if he ever said something like that again and then as if ignoring his cutting remark, she looked at Peggy and took her arm.

"Come on Peggy, let's get down the tube now, find us a nice bed for the night," she said leading them both past the Policeman and off towards the Aldwych station way off in the distance, Gerald allowed himself a small chuckle as they stomped off, he then turned and followed them at a distance until he reached the cut which led up towards Covent Garden and there he left the bright lights of The Strand and his wife to hopefully bring home a few of life's forgotten treats.

Reenie had kept an eye on all this before she'd made her move on Ralph and as she crossed the road, she was hesitant, Ralph was known for being a talker, could she handle him, but as she got to the pavement, Ralph turned around which gave her no time to change her mind and walk on by, he caught her eye.

"Hello precious," he said looking at her straight on, his right eye giving Reenie a small but delicately controlled wink. "Where's the old man gone?" he continued as he looked towards where Gerald had disappeared moments earlier.

Reenie pretended to be shocked and surprised that Ralph was addressing, "Sorry, you talking to me?"

Ralph smiled to himself knowing that she was there because of him. Looking around, he quickly pointed out that there was no one else about, still trying to make out she was there by accident Reenie questioned Ralph why he was talking to her *'as if he knew her and her husband'*. Ralph thought about this for a moment whilst he surreptitiously looked Reenie up and down with an admiring eye.

"I do," he said.

"A copper, ain't he?" she nodded, as if to assure Ralph he'd got the question right.

"Well," he said, "it was me who asked him to bring you here tonight."

Knocked back by this Reenie quickly questioned Ralph, "Oh yeah, why's that then?"

"I saw you the other day with that twit in the underpants,"

he said chuckling to himself, "and I thought to myself, Ralphie my boy, she's a cracker." He paused deliberately, waiting for Reenie to commit to a reply.

She blushed immediately but stayed on the defensive, "That twit, as you put it, is one of my best friends and he happens to be in the hospital at the moment so he can't defend himself." Ralph roared with laughter.

"No, he can't defend himself your right and I bet he's got one hell of a sore arse at the moment."

Hurt, Reenie immediately looked away from Ralph away over his broad shoulder way off into the distance along The Strand, she pursed her lips and paused before looking at Ralph again "How did you know about that?" she asked incredulously, Ralph, shot her a look that said it all.

"I forgot you know it all don't you," she hissed. "Anyway, what is it you want from us?"

Reenie was now in two minds this meeting with Ralph, once, she thought it was probably a good idea, now though, she really wasn't sure, her tone had become terse and even her body language was starting to mirror her thoughts and sensing her displeasure Ralph immediately tried his best to win her back, but in a more calm and considerate style.

Moving in closer he whispered in Reenie's ear, "It's not us, you and him is it!" Smiling he took her hand in his, "It's you I want," he said breathlessly in her ear before he gloriously continued "Do you like chocolate, fruit?" She smiled, blushing ever so slightly at Ralph's directness. "Of course you do," he continued flirtingly, as he lightly ran his fingers over her flushing cheeks, pausing to let Reenie soak up the full effect of his charm he peered longingly into her eyes, gently raking his fingers through the loose strands of her hair that were gently, ever so gently, blowing on the evening air.

Ralph was good, old school, and sensing that she was about to melt he started to offer an explanation of how her husband had him banged to rights down one of the tubes the other evening and that whilst being questioned by him he had come up with an idea that would bring them both closer together whilst he had been bargaining for his freedom.

"So you did a deal with my husband, then!" Reenie was aghast. "And instead of nicking you, he let you go, and then, had the nerve to bring me down here like it's some sort of cattle market!"

Ralph thought about this for a brief second, on the one hand, he didn't want to upset Reenie, but it was too good an opportunity to drop Gerald further into the thick of it,

"Well, that's about the size of it," Ralph said, a smile as wide as the Thames at tower bridge starting to poke its way out from under his magnificent moustache. "You know, I only offered him a bit of fruit, telling him it would probably pep up his home life if you get my drift like." Ralph was seriously playing down his part in the deal-making.

Although she did rather like the man who stood before her, she was incensed at the thought of her husband, Gerald, bargaining with him, using her as the bate. "You wait here!" she scolded at Ralph as she turned and marched in the direction of where Gerald had disappeared towards Covent Garden, upon nearing Southampton Street, the cut-through, Gerald appeared from the street looking very sheepish his eyes darting between Reenie and Ralph who was further back down The Strand in exactly the same spot he started out in earlier that evening when accosted by Peggy and Ethel. But as Reenie approached Gerald, he put his hand up as if submitting as if to stop her from shouting at him, Renee's face was racked with anger, but it was also tinged with an adolescent look of mischief, this was going to be on her terms.

"Gerald!" she bellowed at the top of her voice.

"Before you start, Reen," he replied lowering his hand quickly.

"Before I start! You've got a nerve, Gerald Selby. You didn't tell me you'd arranged this all along."

"I told you to tap him up!" Gerald said, instantly, hesitantly, not sure how Reenie would react, seeing red she slowly started to pull her late husband to bits, with all the witty skill her cockney upbringing would allow, she ranted at Gerald for a full minute, never once giving him the chance to reply, and each time she stopped to catch her breath she raised a solitary finger and roughly prodded it hard on his lips, so he was left knowing exactly her intention. Finally, she stopped and drew a deep breath, there was a long silence punctuated only by the sound of the odd car or bus travelling along The Strand trying to get out of central London before Hitler sent in another wave of the destructive bombers.

"So what did he offer you?" pleaded Gerald, who had by now become like an over-excited teenage child.

"Chocolate!"

"Is that all, you mean all this aggro for a bar of chocolate?"

"No Gerald," Reenie added cattily, "but chocolate is all you're getting out of this; I'm going back over there to do a deal you can wait here and when I'm finished, I'll let you know."

Gerald was now in Renee's hands as well as the spivs! he

116

knew he should have just nicked him the other evening, but Ralph had been so convincing, now here he was, hoping his wife would get him out of this mess and most importantly get him out of trouble.

Trying to take back control, Gerald barked an order at Reenie which he hoped would put him back in the driving seat. "OK, I'll give you five minutes and then I'm coming to get you."

But she had already turned in Ralph's direction and added some much-needed lipstick to brighten her features, this time she meant business, as she glided off over to where Ralph had patiently waited for the return of his princess.

As she got to Ralph, she held out her long slender hand which Ralph immediately took in his, as he did so, he stooped ever so slightly and lifting her hand to meet his lips he gently kissed her skin for the first time. Looking up he caught her gaze, her face had now changed, her features had become softer, and her long blonde hair fell sweetly over both her quaint shoulders. Neither spoke for a moment as they looked into each other's eyes, Ralph couldn't be sure, was she playing with him?

"Gerald doesn't mind you talking to me then?" he inquired sheepishly.

"He has no choice, I'm in charge now," Reenie replied stoically shrugging her shoulders.

"Spirit! I like that in my girls," Ralph said trying to lift the mood.

"I'm one of your girls now then am I?" she said without the merest whiff of irony.

"No...No, that's not what I meant." Ralph was quick to try and get it back on his terms.

"What did you mean then, Ralph?" Reenie was now very much in charge and Ralph was suddenly being put under pressure, this wasn't how he thought it should go, Ralph quick as a flash explained that he preferred ladies who had some fire in their stomachs, ladies who weren't put off by his ways or his cheeky manner. Keeping up the constant chat he could see she was starting to mellow again and so occasionally he would touch her arm letting his hand linger for longer than it should, but just enough time for her to notice or he would move his head from one side to the other so he could catch her gaze and his eyes would twinkle as they met hers, putting her more and more at ease until eventually he paused allowing Reenie her chance to reply, she thought for a short while before saying anything. As she looked into his deep blue eyes she saw her future a long way from where it was now, she saw a new companion, someone who would treat her like a lady or at the very least far better than Gerald had, she saw someone who would treat her to flowers and perfumes and someone who would love her and tell her how nice she looked. Eventually she took his hands, as she pulled Ralph gently towards her and started to whisper into his ear, she told him she liked him, desired him even, and that in a strange sort of way she admired the way the war hadn't deterred his entrepreneurial ways, all the while neither had dropped their gaze on one another, she was in his grips but she also knew that she could control the situation to her benefit as well, she let Ralph carry on talking, she was in awe of him and she loved his smooth cockney voice and the smell of the cologne he was wearing, the cool evenings breeze bought a fresh waft of his aroma every time he shifted his feet and this would rip right through her senses, she was hooked and he knew it, he moved towards her and held out a strong hand and as he did so he gently brushed her long fringe across from left to right revealing her beautiful face to its fullest, Reenie looked at him, urging him to keep talking, as she got up close she sneaked another whiff of Ralph's cologne, the aroma was mesmerizing, Gerald never smelt so sweetly, even on their wedding day it had been as much as she could do to get him to wear some clean pants and a shirt that had seen the underside of an iron, as Ralph felt her breath on his neck he turned ever so slightly just enough so their lips could lightly, softly, delicately touch, but just as he was about to make his move, Ralph caught sight of Gerald marching towards them, the anger in his face was obvious even from that distance and so Ralph immediately stood back, Reenie was hurt but she couldn't see what Ralph could.

"Damn! Here comes your old man," Ralph whispered in her direction, this made Reenie take a step back and turn to face back up the street in the direction of where here errant husband was coming from, she let him get almost to where they were standing.

"Gerald, luvvy, you need to leave me and this nice man alone for the evening." Gerald shook his head shocked at the very suggestion how could he let his wife be seen out on the town with a known villain. It had been a stupid idea and Ralph had got away scot-free.

He couldn't be sure, but from where he'd stood and watched the two of them, Ralph hadn't passed anything of use to Reenie not even a single bar of chocolate or any of the other things that he had promised from the previous evening, no…no, he wasn't going to agree for this to go on any longer he certainly wasn't going to allow him to go off on some random date with his wife, what if his station commander saw them he'd think that he was involved in some kind of villainy *Guilty by association*, he thought to himself.

"You gone out of your mind, girl, I can't leave you alone with a spiv."

"No I haven't gone out of my mind, but I just might if you don't leave me and him alone!" she argued pointing in the direction of Ralph.

Reenie was now wearing a scornful look, one that would make the Ravens move swiftly on from The Tower; Gerald knew that this wasn't going to work in his favour at all.

All their married life she'd been very persuasive she'd always got her way, so he should have thought about that before he agreed with Ralph to bring her along, but if he didn't agree now, she would probably just go anyway, so he had to try and at least make it work, in part, in his favour, he pulled Reenie towards him so Ralph couldn't hear what he was about to say,

"I don't like this; I don't like this one bit!"

Reenie assured him that Ralph was a good man and that he did have some 'special things!' just for him, but, that she needed to go off with Ralph to finalise the deal. Gerald thought long and hard before he reluctantly agreed to let her go, but it would have to be in exchange for some of Ralphs spoils, the thought of chocolate and maybe a fresh banana again was too much for the under-pressure copper to ignore, and a massive distraction from what he knew was right. Regrettably Gerald stood aside and let Reenie move towards Ralph, as he did so she gave her new suitor a knowing wink, a wink so that her new man would then know that Gerald was in agreement, neither man spoke a word as Ralph put his hand into his long dark coat and started to pull out some of his goods to make peace with Gerald.

Across the street from where this strange collaboration was taking place, Paddy and Ardle were lurking in one of the many grand doorways that made up The Strand in all its finery, they had both been following Ralph since the previous evening's kerfuffle and when he'd returned to his house at the rough end of Portland Road in Notting hill they were still tracking their man, but it was late and so they had both bedded down in the area that night, in one of the many bombed-out properties that lined the Portland Road, the next morning they rose bright and early to catch up with their man, but first they sneaked a couple of pints of milk from the dairy a few hundred yards further along Portland Road from where they had stayed that night.

Ralph's dad had worked in the very same dairy which meant he had links with the old gipsy camps that had been there since before the turn of the century. Ralph had grown up amongst these gipsies and he now saw himself as one of them, a business man, not the usual type that put on a suit, and conformed to the nine to five routine of the city, but more as one of the Gypsy types who could earn their living from buying and selling, by using their initiative, their cheek, their witty banter, he'd never had a proper job like his dad and as a child he'd watched his mother and father struggle, so as he became an adult he'd gone out and earned himself a place in local folklore buying, selling and conning his way through life much to his dads approval as they never wanted for anything again.

Ralph always managed to put a joint of meat on the table every Sunday for lunch something his dad was never able to do on his meagre wage, his mum saw it differently though and she so wanted him to be known for something more worthwhile, in her mind, rather than for being quick on his toes when the law were around but this was turning into his finest hour he was sure she'd be proud especially if he managed to take the beautiful Reenie home to meet her.

Ardle and Paddy had then caught back up with Ralph when he'd started to walk back towards his patch earlier this evening and had watched the growing tension between husband and wife evolve, and as Gerald stood aside and let his wife eagerly stroll off arm in arm with the lucky spiv, Paddy turned to his travelling companion and said, "Now that puts a different angle on it."

"Hmmm," replied Ardle. "Well, we'll just have to nick the stuff ourselves."

Paddy looked to the floor and shook his head, as Ardle, blissfully unaware of what this meant, nodded his eagerly in the general direction of where Ralph had stood some minutes earlier.

***

Josey and his gang of kids had earlier managed to get away from all their parents, that afternoon, many of the 'older' parents had been catching up on some much needed sleep after their fretful nights sheltering at different destinations around town and the younger parents, well, they were always too busy to keep an eye on them, but Josey, had made them all promise their parents, that they would meet up with them again down in the tube at The Aldwych before any bombings started again, that way it would keep the olds of their tails until the early evening at the very least, so they had hours to go before that time of day came lumbering back around and so therefore after a small debate, whilst they were all stood round the burning embers of a bombed out building in The Kingsbury Road, they found themselves exactly where they said they wouldn't go again, back in the old disused tunnel that they had been shown the previous evening. This time though Ralph was not with them and they all felt particularly good about that as they sat around on all the old boxes and crates that housed all the treasures that Ralph had been eager to show them the previous evening.

None of them had said anything for a while, they just sat there and soaked up the environment, most of them only too glad to be away from their pushy, protective parents, but it was cold and damp down there, a world away from the late summer afternoons they were experiencing outside in the real world and the lightweight clothing they all had on made them shiver as the wind whistled nonstop through the confines of the old tunnel complex.

Slimey, as usual, was always the first to speak when there had been an enforced silence among the gang and today was going to be no different, looking towards Josey as their leader to come up with some form of entertainment, he barked out loudly to be heard from his seat further back down the tunnel.

"Here Josey, what are we going to do tonight?"

Immediately, Josey snapped back, "Why, you bored?"

"I am," said Knock Knees who was sitting quietly about three feet from Josey on a small orange box stuffed with old woolly blankets to protect whatever it was that was sitting in the bottom of the box. Josey couldn't believe his ears, his mob of ramshackle kids were starting to revolt, and he needed to crush the rebellion before it started to get any legs.

"What's wrong with you lot, we're having the time of our lives aren't we, all this is ours, no one knows what we're doing."

It was hardly a speech that would've spurred a generation of like-minded kids and as Josey looked around at the ramshackle bunch of war-weary young souls he realised that most of them did still look as though they needed a real adventure. He needed to think a bit harder and so they all sat there again in total silence, only the occasional gust of wind blowing up the tunnel caused by the trains passing round the network further up the tracks where the underground was still a booming industry, would break their silence.

Slimey was again the first speak but this time there was a little more desperation in his voice as he looked up at the other children who were all still sat down with their heads slumped into their hands, none of them moving, just occasionally kicking out at a piece of rubbish blown into their pathway.

"Smells down here and I'm still hungry!" he moaned loudly as he stood up from his orange crate. Four Eyes had never been a fan of Slimey's and she shot a glance at Josey raising her eyes in mock surprise.

She then snapped back at Slimey, "You only ever think about your belly."

"No, I don't," Slimey whined.

"Yes, you do," Four Eyes said resolutely. Four Eye's statement became the catalyst for them all to start having their say and as all the gang started to chip in and moan at Slimey, a general argument started to escalate. Slimey wasn't listening though and eventually he stood up on the biggest stack of crates he could find, a little bit back from the main group, but close enough so he could be heard, preparing himself to speak he drew himself up to all his 'three feet – six inches' in height, cleared his throat and spat the black snotty contents out into the darkness towards the old track and then as loudly as he could he started to make his point, hoping they would all listen.

"Well, I haven't eaten anything for ages!" he shouted at the top of his little voice. "Not anything proper!"

The argument quickly abated as all of the assembled gang stopped and looked around at Slimey standing tall and proud above them all, Josey chuckled to himself, Slimey was not the tallest person in the gang, and he was also never usually the one to get up and want his side heard first, they all stood in stunned silence their chins seemingly stuck to the floor!

Charlie the tallest member of the gang thought about what Slimey had said.

"Ahem," he said just loud enough to be heard in the cold windy tunnel, usually Charlie said nothing, as he felt a bit of an outsider coming as he did from the Posher end of Portland Road W11, he'd met the other members of the gang on some of the rough sites around the city when he'd sneaked off from his parents during an argument one night two years previously and even though he was a firm part of the gang now he always felt that he never quite fitted in, but now, 'he' had something to tell, something that they just might be interested in, so Charlie felt at long last it was his turn to have his say.

"I know where we can get something to eat."

The gang all stopped what they were doing and immediately looked up at where Charlie was stood.

"I was up by that big hotel on the Strand the other night, I

125

got in the kitchens."

There was an audible sharp intake of breath from the gang as they heard what he'd done, none of them had ever been quite that brave before after all it was The Savoy, no one went anywhere near that place unless they had film star money and then, as they had all discussed once, you would probably only be able to afford a cup of tea and one biscuit! They all looked at each other not quite knowing what to say in reply.

"It's alright, no one saw me." He added, quickly realising they were all just a bit worried that he'd overstepped the mark, he went on, "Oh, it was lovely. I nicked a plate of cooked meat."

Rubbing his stomach he stopped for maximum effect as he remembered the cold cooked meats he's been able to feast on, slowly miming to the others how he picked up the meat and ate it slice by beautiful slice, he explained in great detail what each portion was like, just as his father had done many times before when all they sat down for the family's Sunday lunch, Charlie started with a huge slab of beef.

"Cooked," he said, "until the juices ran free."

Each glorious mouthful spilling its cold blood-red gravy down young Charlie's chin, furiously he dabbed his chin with the end of his tattered sleeve trying to blot the liquid before it fell to the floor and betrayed his stolen position in the confines of the grand hotel's kitchens. Quickly he moved onto a mouthful of cold lamb 'pink and cooked to perfection' its layers of cold fat had hardened into a creamy white paste. Charlie shivered as he dreamt of huge mounds of crisp roasted potatoes and lashings of gravy and a splash of mint sauce to wash it all down, pausing, he licked his lips for more effect and then he moved onto a massive portion of cold roasted chicken sliced perfectly from the bird, before finishing with a slice of cooked pork that had been brushed with huge dollops of cold sweet apple sauce, all the children were captivated and Charlie had them in the palm of his hand until he finished with his bombshell.

"Made me sick though!"

Four Eyes, who was ever the argumentative one, couldn't resist and told Charlie sharply that the meat was probably off.

"No, it wasn't," scorned Charlie as he explained that he'd probably just scoffed it all down a bit too quickly.

Slimey who was still stood tall and proud on his pile of crates immediately tried to take over and become the leader for the night, telling the assembled gang that they should all take Charlie's lead and go to the hotel and get themselves some of what Charlie had sampled days earlier, the gang look eager to do this, but Charlie looked on, shaking his head.

"Hold up," he said. It was after all Charlie that had found it and Charlie quite rightly was insistent that it should be him that said whether they should go back or not. They all stood and thought about what he had just said whilst they shuffled their feet from side to side, some of them chewing the insides of their cheeks, looking guilty, muttering to themselves and each other, they'd always done things they shouldn't do and shared the experiences among them, they were a gang after all, why should Charlie say whether they can have some of his fun, why shouldn't they have some of his fun? Finally, after several minutes of silence and lots of nodding and finger-pointing Josey rightfully took the lead knocking Slimey off the box he'd proudly stood on for the last ten minutes, he himself stood tall making them all aware who the boss was.

"Charlie's right," he said. "We can't all just go belting up there."

Slimey who had now picked himself up from the pile of blankets that Josey had knocked him into wasn't happy that he had been unceremoniously dislodged from his perch on high, or the fact that he'd gone against him and said they couldn't go and get some of the cooked meats, Slimey let out a huge huff which made them all turn and look at him.

Josey thought it best that he finished what he had intended saying, "If we all go belting up there, we'll get caught…no we got to think about this one."

Slimey who was still smarting from being dumped on his backside by Josey, thought it best they ask Ralph as he'd know exactly what they should do, but Josey was having none of it and told them all what he thought of Ralph and that he didn't want to talk to him again as he thought he was an 'idiot'. Four Eyes looked at Josey with a frown as he questioned him, he'd thought they all had got on with Ralph, what did Josey suddenly mean?

"Well," said Josey adopting a pose with one hand on his hip and the other bent as if his wrist had become limp, looking like he was a teapot, he went on. "Don't you find him a bit strange?" he said with a chuckle to himself.

Slimey caught on straight away and started to get silly, walking up and down the platform mirroring Josey's pose, as he did so the others just looked on without saying a thing before he stopped, realising what an idiot he looked like.

Taking a deep breath Slimey coughed into his fisted hand and tried to make himself look a bit more serious before he asked Josey in a very grown-up manner, if, he thought Ralph was a poof, eagerly Four Eyes joined in saying that he thought he was! Quickly, he urged the others to agree with him but

Charlie, very much the thinker of the group, said that he didn't walk like one. They all became quiet again as they thought about what Charlie had said. Slimey broke the silence first again and offered that you didn't have to walk like one, to be one.

Charlie nodded and then spoke as if he was full of knowledge on this topic, "My father reckons he knows a poof who lives down our road."

Four Eyes was eager to know how his dad knew, which made the rest of the gang on a mass turn to Charlie and ask the same question, "How?"

Sitting in somewhat seclusion away from all the others and against the far wall were Little Jenny and Kate two sisters whose house had been bombed out some days earlier in the Mile End Road. Josey had given special permission for them to join the gang tonight on this particular jaunt into the unknown, being a bit shy, the two girls hadn't really joined in with all the speculation about the hotel and the food or Ralph, they didn't usually go out, as they were only just old enough for their mums to allow them a bit more freedom but they'd listened to all the stories the other gang members told when bedding down previously in the main tunnel and thought it would be fun to join them, without their parents knowing, they'd both seen Ralph doing his bit outside the station, when arriving previously for a nights shelter and he was always good to the younger ones giving them the odd boiled sweet or sliver of chocolate when their mums weren't watching, so Jenny spoke up for him, much to Kate's astonishment and told them all to shut up, as she thought he was 'nice'. Four Eyes ever being the joker asked her if she meant Charlie's dad.

"No," she said pulling a face. "Ralph, you fools."

Kate quickly told Jenny to be quite and shut up as they had just got in with the gang and shouldn't spoil things on the first outing and so after that they all sat in silence again pondering Ralphs masculinity and watching the rodents scampering up and down the old tracks. Occasionally one of them would throw a screwed up ball of paper or card at them trying to knock them off the rail, Slimey had thrown several not hitting his target once before he'd grown to curious of their previous conversation about the hotel.

"Well, what about all that grub up there, what we going to do about it?" he muttered almost to himself, Josey who was still sitting atop the biggest stack of crates jumped up quickly, startling all the children as he did so, holding his arms out as if he were carrying a rifle.

"We'll attack it like the army do!" he commanded, much to everyone's amusement, except Charlie who as usual had taken on board what Josey had said and then turned it round into a more serious implication.

"Where are we going to get a tank from?" he said. Josey fell about laughing.

"Don't be stupid, Charlie, no, we got to think about this one, that's what I mean." Charlie looked at Josey with a glint in his young eye as he tapped the side of his nose as if to indicate to Josey he was no fool!

The discussion on the hotel's kitchen went on for ages, as back and forth each would offer a way or means of them all getting into the hotel without being caught so they could feast on any or all of the many delicacies that may have been left about unwittingly in the kitchens and all the while none of the children saw or heard Ardle and Paddy creeping stealthily onto the old platform.

Both Ardle and Paddy had run like the wind from the doorway in which they'd spied Ralph and Reenie going off together, they had both thought Ralph would immediately be bringing Reenie down the tube to show her all the treasures that he had found and that the two of them would get the best of what was on offer before anybody else could get their hands on it.

Even though they'd made quite a bit of noise descending the flights of stairs down into the gloom and had burst onto the platform in a dreadful hurry the children had been far too busy arguing about the hotel and things that they hadn't noticed, so as they made themselves at home in their now familiar hiding place, they kept an eager eye on all the treasure as well as the entrance on to the platform in case Ralph and Reenie suddenly made an appearance, hoping that the children would get bored and disappear quickly to leave them to root around and find the best stuff to take for themselves. Settling in they were both on edge, "After all" Ardle said, "We may need to be quick to lay claim ourselves, Ralph might come back at some point!"

Back along the platform, Jenny was fidgeting around on her stack like a bee on a honey pot and all the while complaining that what she was sitting on, hurt, as it was all pointy!

Kate grabbed her hand and whispered sharply in her ear to stop complaining, it was after all their first adventure with the gang, telling her not to spoil it for them, before adding "Just sit still or just don't sit on it at all." Kate was furious that Jenny might spoil things.

"But there's nowhere else to sit," Jenny told her, a tear was now forming in the corner of her eye; she sniffed to herself and tried to wiggle into a more comfortable spot. Kate had had enough.

"Find out what you're sitting on then," she huffed loudly in Jenny's general direction.

Jenny jumped up to satisfy, not only her own need to know what she was sitting on but to try and pacify Kate for a minute. She pulled back the pile of blankets that had been placed neatly over the top of the box and was immediately transfixed, her pupils wide and straining as she stared at what was before her in the box.

"Guns!" she exclaimed barely able to move or speak, as they had not been with them the night before, Jenny and Kate were unaware of what the rest of them had seen the previous time they had been down there, and the gang hadn't going to be forthcoming in front of all the oldies about it.

"Loads of them," she went on transfixed by the gleaming metal, all neatly stored in the box before her.

"This isn't good all this stuff down 'ere," Kate said looking for support from the others, as they all started to gather around.

Josey had his thinking head-on and looking concerned he told the gathered throng that it would be best if they all made their way out of there and up onto The Strand where they could have a clearer idea on how they were all going to get themselves some supper. Four Eyes was way ahead of the gang and already running and stumbling her way up the stairs in the gloom towards the fresher air outside, as she got to within a flight of stairs from the top she was thrown forward knocked completely off her feet by the almighty explosion that took place beneath her, the rumble that reverberated around the tunnels seemed to go on forever and as she lay there in the darkness a huge cloud of smoke billowed up the stairway engulfing her and depriving her lungs of much-needed oxygen, she scrambled to her feet, her small lungs heaving as they cried out for some fresh air to fill them. As she continued on up to The Strand her mind was full of what she had seen and eventually heard, she could only hope that the rest had already got out as she wasn't turning back to find out. She burst through the old rusty corrugated iron that had been placed strategically over the entrance to the old station years ago to stop people going in.

She staggered in to the road desperately gasping for some fresh air. As she stood there, she was oblivious as small pieces of debris fell around her from the buildings above the old station and crashed into the road, she stood and waited for the others to appear for what seemed like an age but no one appeared, as she slowly began to catch her breath she ran back across to the battered iron barrier and pulled it back towards her, as she peered in she called their names out slowly and precisely, one at a time, but she didn't hear a thing, she tried once more, much louder this time, but again she heard nothing, instinctively she knew she had to get back to the adults in the shelter at The Aldwych and tell them what had happened, if she was going to get into trouble then so be it, her friends were way more important than a good leathering from her dads best Sunday belt. She'd felt that before, after she got caught nicking some milk from old Andrew's float one morning, when she was desperate for something to drink after trying her first cigarette, everyone had goaded her into inhaling the cigarette and she'd sucked so hard on it the smoke had become red hot, she'd coughed and heaved so much that morning that she was desperate for something to ease her throat and when she'd spotted the old man's milk float still on its early morning deliveries unattended, she swiped two bottles but old man Andrews had seen her as he was coming out of the back alley, he'd been in delivering to Mrs Murphy the old nurse who'd delivered her mum and dad back in the day and as she stood there guzzling one of the bottles he'd leapt at her and she'd made such a racket that Mrs Murphy had come out to find out what all the commotion was about and she told Andrew's who her parents were, he'd then marched round to see them after he'd finished his round later that day and he'd told her mum and dad. She winced as she remembered the pain of her dads belt as it connected with her backside and how it had made her cry for at least an hour but she had to tell them, her friends were probably in serious trouble she'd have to face the consequences.

She took off in the direction of the Aldwych station as fast as her scrawny little legs would carry her, a ginger cat ran out from a doorway, as she approached, the cat let out a huge squeal and almost leapt at Four Eyes as she tried to scramble past, nearly sending her tumbling face-first into the cold concrete London Street, but she kept up the pace all the way there, briefly stopping as she got to the station's entrance she took a long deep breath and prepared herself to go down into the tunnel to find the adults and let them know what had just happened.

Back in the old station as the clouds of smoke and dust settled Ardle rolled to one side and rubbed some of the dust off his face he coughed loudly and tried to clear his throat, hacking up dirty sooty black phlegm, wincing from the agonising pain he felt in his left leg, he reached down and pushed some of the debris from the blast to one side freeing up his ankles so he could at least move his feet again, the darkness in the tunnel was now all consuming and as Ardle looked around he couldn't see if his friend was still there, he called out twice to Paddy but heard nothing, he rolled onto his front and pulled himself up onto his knees wincing from the shear pain he felt drive through his body, slowly, very slowly he moved around the area feeling with his hands all around him, nothing, just lumps of concrete and broken brick the pain in his lower legs was indescribable so he shifted himself into a position that was more comfortable, lying there he closed his eyes, there was no sound coming from anywhere, slowly he drifted off.

***

Alice had tried hard to find Connie all day, she'd visited all their usual haunts and asked around for her but she hadn't been seen at any of them and now she was worried, especially as she knew she'd gone off with Charlie and that alone had caused her some anxiety. Charlie wasn't her usual type of beau for one he didn't talk like them and he was a scruffy man who didn't appear to work and she didn't know where he supposedly lived, even if she did, she was sure Connie wouldn't have gone there alone, she thought about it and figured that if they were still together then she must have taken him to a hotel somewhere near to The Strand and the station where they had last been seen leaving together, but where? all the places she would normally visit wouldn't have let Charlie into the foyer, let alone up the stairs to any of the rooms, unless of course they had thought that he was there to do some maintenance. It didn't sit well with her at all and she was still fretting later that day as she decided to make the trip down into the tunnel at the Aldwych station, as she sat there on her makeshift bed she got out a copy of The Times and lost herself in the news from around the world, occasionally looking up and saying hello to people as they all started gathering down there for safety, from time to time she would be bumped or pushed as people squeezed past much to her annoyance, especially as Connie wasn't there for them to fret together. But as the evening wore on she was actually really starting to settle in and had chatted to most of those people that were around her and had found them a really friendly bunch, some had even offered her sandwiches made from whatever they had managed to lay their hands on and she'd tried them with good grace, even though as she'd chewed into them she had wanted to gag at the taste, Haslet in particular was one she didn't like the taste of even though the others all found it a particular treat.

She had managed to bring in a few things herself and offered some of her apples around that she'd managed to pick up earlier when looking for Connie around Covent Garden, little did Alice know Connie and Charlie had actually been close by to her first thing this morning as they had been holed up in the flat in Drury Lane since the previous night, making the most of their time together. Connie had actually popped out for some supplies as soon as the markets opened up but had worn some darkened glasses and a brightly knitted shawl that she'd found in the flat high up over her head so she couldn't be recognised. Charlie had stayed put whilst she went out; she felt it better that way as it would probably have been way too obvious the two of them walking around together. Staying behind Charlie had thought to himself that morning whilst Connie had been out, and now he knew what he had to do, he was going to get involved in the war effort the moment they decided to go public about their affair.

Winnie spotted Alice as soon as she entered the station and was very keen to find out where Charlie had disappeared to the previous evening, she made her way up the platform boldly to where Alice was sitting and sat down on a pile of old blankets putting her bags on the ground she appeared to make herself at home for the evening, Alice was chuckling away to herself following a conversation she'd just had with the old gentleman in the flat cap who was sat directly behind her, as Winnie finished sorting all her stuff out Alice lent forward and tapped her brazenly on the shoulder.

"I say," she said, Alice always seemed to speak in a posh condescending style, "I'm rather starting to enjoy coming down here with you lot since my friend is not spending much time with me."

Unaware that Alice also was in the dark as to the whereabouts of the love-struck duo, Winnie saw this as her chance to find out where Charlie had disappeared to.

"Well, I wouldn't worry about her as she seems to have taken a liking to our Charlie boy." Winnie was expecting Alice to tell all and to let her know where the two of them had gone but Alice knew as little as Winnie.

"I am worried," she said, which caused Winnie some concern, Alice could see it and tried to allay her concern although she put her foot right in it. "Well, she is from a different class!"

"Oooh get you," Winnie countered sharply but Alice chuckled as she knew she had her own 'different' place in society and reminded Winnie that Connie also had a certain

137

pedigree that she must adhere to, this didn't sit well with the larger-than-life cockney who prided herself on being able to communicate with all classes and Winnie wasn't about to let some high-class girl from the out-of-town start putting her and Charlie down.

"So what you're saying is, our Charlie's a mongrel!"

Alice sighed, she didn't have her confidant with her and knew that if a full-blown argument was about to start, she was likely to come off second best to the fiery East End woman. "Well, I hope he looks after her that's all," she said, trying to politely defuse the situation.

Having decided that they ought to show their faces again Charlie and his new partner, made their way from the cosy flat in Drury Lane, where they had spent so much of the day together, over to the station.

Once at platform level they started picking their way slowly through the assembled mass of Londoners. Eventually they found themselves stood by Alice and Winnie, just as things were about to get heated.

Alice spoke first directing her conversation at Connie, She made out to Connie that she'd missed her earlier and wanted to know where she'd been? This unsettled Connie.

They had been friends for longer than she cared to think, and to her, it was obvious that Connie was going to try to start spinning a tale, she was also cross at her friend for leaving yesterday without saying anything, especially with a man who was clearly not her usual sort and one who was outside their social class and that she was worried for her reputation "You have to think about that" she said "It's no good galivanting around London with...well with the lower classes" she whispered to Connie, hoping that Winnie or Charlie didn't hear. Amused at what Connie had said Alice told her she was a snob as they'd had fun and that Charlie was cute "In a common sort of way"

Alice was not going to agree with her friend on this and told her so, she said that Charlie was common and that he was dirty and that he smelt and that he should be doing something for the war effort "Didn't he know that?"

Winnie had overheard the girls' discussion and as it involved her Charlie, she wasn't going to let her thoughts on the matter go without them being heard. "Of course, he knows it," she barked at the two socialites. "At least, he knows his own kind, not like you Hampstead lot. You're all inbred. No wonder you talk like you got something caught in your throats."

"They're plums, dear," Connie said sarcastically. Winnie's rugged face was quick to show that she was starting to get up a head of steam, but unlike Alice, Connie knew only too well how to handle situations like these. For years, she'd sung in music halls all over the country and had virtually represented herself, going up against unscrupulous theatre managers on a daily basis to make sure she'd got what she was rightfully owed after a night singing to 'their' paying customers.

"Well 'ent you lucky you can afford a plum," Winnie quickly countered, not to be outdone. Connie quickly told her that they would probably make her sick. Winnie stood abruptly, hands on hips and snarling like a caged animal she came straight back telling Connie that it was the 'two of them that made her sick', coming down the tube station for shelter with their airs and graces, 'born with a silver spoon in their mouths'. Belittling them some more, she went on, "Never done a day's work, well not proper work. Champagne for breakfast, caviar for dinner." Most of Winnie's rant amused Connie, and she stood there all the while with a wry smile on her face.

"Lobster for tea, please don't forget that," she added sarcastically, pausing before she spoke again, she needed everyone present to hear what she wanted to say next, she needed everyone to know how she felt, even if it was aimed at the scowling Londoner in front of her.

"You really are a short sighted, ungrateful, foul-mouthed person. You don't know Alice or me, we're suffering just like you. Don't you understand?" Alice pulled Connie to one side she knew what Connie was trying to say, but Winnie was in such a bad mood that it would have been lost on her.

"I wouldn't bother, Connie. Her sort never understand. She just thinks she can get her own way by just shouting and hollering."

Sitting down on Alice's makeshift bed, Connie was now in a reflective mood and she told Alice, that she thought, that Winnie needed teaching a lesson, and that if 'she' lost something that was dear to her or someone, she would understand how they all needed to stick together.

"After all, there was a war on, in case she didn't know." Just as Connie finished her sentence, an almighty boom of an explosion somewhere shattered the evening air of the tube station and the odd flake of dusty concrete loosened from the tube ceiling and fell amongst them. "See what I mean!" said Connie, not at all bothered by the blast, Alice and Connie's conversation continued, nobody at all seemed worried by the explosion as it echoed through the tunnels of the Piccadilly Line.

"Of course, these people know there's a war on otherwise they wouldn't be hundreds of feet underground sleeping on a cold floor with some smelly oik for a pillow. Connie what's wrong with you?" Alice argued some more.

"Oh, I'm fed up with people like her. Most of these people are fun to be with," Connie said as she nodded distastefully in Winnie's direction.

"I know," said Alice, before adding, that's why she thought Winnie's ways were so infuriating. "We've' lived without a care in the world for so long. These people have endured hardship like this even before the war." As Alice finished speaking, Connie had dragged Charlie over to the bed she had already made out of two old suitcases, an orange crate and some old woollen blankets which smelled heavily of naphtha from long gone mothballs that had been stored within them at some point years since. As she teased Charlie, she pushed him to sit down on the makeshift bed sneaking a brief kiss. As she did so, Winnie was aghast as she saw it!

Infuriated, she yelled out, "Charlie!"

"What?" he called back his cheeks ever so slightly flushed.

"You won't go to heaven!" Winnie barked abruptly at Charlie, from where she had spied his romantic union with the upper-class socialite.

No more was said by anybody for the next few minutes and life went on around them as it normally did, games of cards were started and finished an impromptu sing-along started and all the while Charlie knew he had to tell Winnie something, something very important,

"Win," Charlie spoke, in a soft tone towards his oldest friend, he had something important to tell her and he needed her to remain calm. "She's convinced me to join up," he whispered, hoping that Winnie would find this great news. Winnie was incensed.

"Oh cheers," she said shaking her head from side to side looking disgusted at Charlie as she did so, Charlie hung his head.

He knew that wasn't all Winnie was going to say on the matter and he was right, Winnie hadn't finished, she continued to bellow at him, letting him know how 'infuriated' she was, that after all these years she'd known him, some 'posh sort' from out-of-town swans into his life and all of a sudden the 'conscientious objector' in him changes and he bleeding well 'joins up'.

"Oh, do behave!" Connie brusquely sneered at Winnie.

She was not going to let her get away with another rant at her expense and proceeded to tell Winnie that Charlie only needed a good shove in the right direction and if she'd listened to him instead of always shouting and hollering, she'd have realised that he wasn't actually against joining up. It was just that he needed to know that if he did, he would be making a difference somewhere.

Winnie immediately turned her nose up at Connie and waved her old yellow headscarf menacingly in her face, whilst not making contact with Connie, it let her know that Winnie was now eager for things to get physical, if, 'she' wanted.

"What is it with you lot!" she bellowed furiously at the pair of girls, who were now squirming in their makeshift bunks due to all the attention they had attracted from all the shouting.

"He's more your sort." Winnie deliberately picked out someone else to face the brunt of her anger and Tim had just wandered back down the tunnels again for a night's shelter.

This time though, Tim hadn't spoken with anyone up at street level as he'd decided to keep his presence rather more anonymous, especially after his run-in with Ralph the previous evening when he'd paid for a non-existent ticket in the non-smoking zone of the platform, where he was now being dragged back into the heat of an argument when all he wanted to do was keep his head down and read his copy of that evening's news.

Winnie moved alongside the poor fellow, by now he was sitting with his back to the huge, curved wall, covering one of the large cigarette adverts at the back of the platform, and she was pulling hard at his arm trying desperately to get him to stand up so that Connie could see who she meant. Tim struggled for a bit before the big lady tired of his reluctance to stand and so she just continued her rant pointing at the hapless man telling all that would listen that Tim was perfect for her as 'he' had all his Ps and Qs in the right place'. If they knew what she meant, Connie answered her without standing. She told Winnie that she knew exactly what she meant but Charlie was 'different'.

"Oh, he's different all right. He ain't got no money for a start!" roared Winnie. This time she was laughing, the two girls sat there, pouting, more than just a little deflated.

Four Eyes stood on the bottom step of the platform entrance trying to spot a familiar face in the crowd. She suddenly spied Winnie further down the platform, the big girl was still standing over the two socialites basking in the glory of her last comment gleefully laughing and mocking them. Four Eyes dashed over towards Winnie, pushing fiercely past everyone in her mad rush to get to her. Four Eyes was terrified, but she had to let her know what had happed down in the disused tunnel, she got to Winnie and tugged firmly on the old gal's tunic desperately trying to get her attention.

Winnie was furious that someone was trying to interfere. She was deeply engrossed in her argument with Connie and Alice and as she turned around to give whatever or whoever it was pulling at her tunic a piece of her mind.

Four Eyes let rip screaming at the top of her voice "Quick! It's Knock Knees, Slimey and Josey."

Tim's eyes widened immediately. "Blimey," he said. "They've got a zoo down here as well." His observation didn't go down at all well. It was clearly obvious something drastic had happened for Four Eyes to be so upset

"Shut up, you imbecile," shouted Alice.

Elsie the old lady rushed her way over to where Four Eyes was standing.

"What's the problem, dear?" she urged. Four Eyes was sobbing and in a daze, desperate to share with them what had gone on.

"We…we…we were up in tunnel three and I…I…it's all gone off!" she stumbled.

"What's gone off?" Elsie asked trying desperately to dry the little girl's tears; Four Eyes composed herself.

"Bombs and st…stuff."

Charlie looked at the little crying girl with a puzzled frown.

"What's she talking about bombs and stuff?" he said. "Why would there be any bombs in the tunnels?"

Sauntering along the platform from the far end, Ralph and Reenie had snuck into the station undetected and on hearing all the commotion Four Eyes was causing, Ralph realised that the small child must have been talking about the tunnel where he had taken the children the night before.

Ralph knew he should step forward and tell all of them that he had taken the children into the old tunnel the previous night and what they had seen, but he also knew they would be horrified at the thought, Ralph quickly whispered to Reenie, what Four Eyes were talking about was where her Gerald had caught him and he was sure there was a good possibility that everything would come out about his bribing Gerald, all they could do was stand there and watch.

Quickly realising that this was a desperate situation Ralph let go of Reenie's lovingly manicured hand, straightened his trilby, brushed down his jacket and stepped forward towards where Four Eyes and the rest were congregating, clearing his throat Ralph tried to speak loudly over all the commotion attempting to sound as official as he could.

"She's probably right," he said. "I was up there the other night and found a store of guns and ammo."

Most of the people gathered on the platform were aware of Ralph's dodgy past. There was a stunned silence. Ralph was on edge, he'd started the ball rolling and needed to get everyone backing him as quickly as possible. Charlie had been stood with his back to Ralph, but he knew the spiv of old. Charlie quickly turned and looked at Ralph sneering at the once cocky spiv, Charlie shook his head.

"And what were you doing there?" Charlie asked.

Ralph quickly saw an opportunity to explain the situation from his point of view.

"It was like another world in all the disused tunnels," he said adding that he'd been round most of the tunnels on the central line and that he'd seen everything, museums, armament stores and meetings taking place. "You name it," he said. "It all goes on down here day and night." Ralph had got himself on a roll as he tried to explain away his reasons for knowing about the 'bombs and stuff'.

"You're mad, son," Charlie sneered at the spiv's knowledge of the underground network, Ralph shrugged his shoulders, he couldn't care less.

But Ralph was quick to snap back, "You don't believe me?" He took a quick glance at all those gathered there he could still see anger in their eyes, he quickly spoke again this time almost imploring them "I'm telling you! I've seen it all with me own eyes." Still there was silence, Four Eyes shuffled uneasily on her feet the tears still flowing freely down her dirt-encrusted cheeks, Elsie put a firm arm around the visibly shaking child and decided to take charge, she looked at Charlie and Ralph in turn and then directed her conversation between the two of them.

"All right, you two idiots, what are we going to do about the children?" Ralph looked at Charlie before he spoke. Sensing that whatever he said wasn't going to appease the assembled throng, stooping so he could speak to Four Eyes on her level, Ralph asked the small child where the problem was. She didn't move a muscle and she remained awkwardly silent. Ralph knew his next question would open a huge can of worms, but it had to be asked.

He took a deep breath and asked Four Eyes, "Is it where we were the other night?" Waiting for the fallout, Ralph stood up and caught Reenie's gaze she raised an eyebrow and bit at her lips.

"Blimey," Charlie sneered. "He's a nonce as well as a spiv." In a flash, Charlie had removed his old woollen jacket and had rolled up his sleeves. Ralph couldn't move, he was hemmed in by the crowd and Charlie was raging as he moved towards Ralph. His fists clenched in anger, Ralph put his arms up trying to avoid the inevitable clout, Charlie took a swing at him but missed and his wild swing glanced off the back of Winnie's shoulder as she'd tried to move between the warring pair. Tim, by now, had managed to escape from where Winnie had pinned him against the back wall and he was now well placed to see everything that was going on.

"Marvellous," he said in his beautifully received accent. "It looks like there is going to be a fight." Shoving Tim aside, Alice stood to her feet, and knocked Tim's smile from his face as she blasted him for being a moron, giving him another almighty shove she pushed him back into the crowd in the general direction of where he started from.

Charlie again took another wild swing at Ralph, this time it was more on target and Ralph had to duck back fast as Charlie's fist missed his pointed nose by a whisker. Connie made a grab for Charlie from behind, her small frame nowhere big enough to stretch her arms around Charlie's middle to hold him back. Winnie, though, stood her ground between the two of them, her presence enough to keep another barrage of fists from flying loosely around between them. Reenie had now got herself through the throng and was stood by Ralph urging him to keep still. Ralph didn't attempt to challenge Charlie. A mortified Four Eyes screamed at the top of her voice, everything stopped and all eyes turned to her.

"It's up just beyond where we were the other night!" she shouted in Ralphs direction. "We found another pile of guns and stuff." Winnie and the others stood there dubious of the young girls last statement. Four Eyes could suddenly feel their anger brewing. "We didn't touch anything, but it all went off....honest." The crowd remained silent, Four Eyes spoke again this time though there was more urgency in her voice, "Some of the kids have been buried in all the rubble." She didn't know if that bit was true, she hoped it wasn't the case but she'd been too afraid to go back and see, Ralph stepped forward and took his moment, taking charge.

"OK!" he shouted so everyone could hear on the platform. "Let's get ourselves organised."

Turning back to Four Eyes he told her that she would need to lead the way, he pointed off in the direction of the tunnel entrance further down the station, then as the two of them moved towards the tracks he told the rest he wanted all the guys and some of the girls to follow them and that someone should also let the police and the home guard know what had happened with that he clambered down onto the tracks turned and lifted Four Eyes down and then signalling to the rest of the mob the pair started to head off towards Tunnel number three, Charlie and Winnie stood there, open-mouthed at what had just happened but as Connie and Alice climbed down onto the tracks to follow the flamboyant spiv Winnie signalled, that, they should also put their trust in him and follow the others into the darkened tunnels.

***

Poor Alby was lying, in a daze, face down on the makeshift hospital bed in the stark, cold, temporary ward that had been set up in the working man's club just off of White Chapel Road following the hospitals direct hit from a Nazi bomb, the room stank of unwashed Londoners and stale blood, all seeking urgent medical attention at the hands of the overworked nurses, some of whom hadn't worn the starched uniform and little cap for years since their retirement.

Alby was by now feeling incredibly sorry for himself. He chewed heavily on his knuckles due to the excruciating pain that was emanating from his backside, the dog had ravaged a large amount of flesh before eventually letting go of Alby the previous night, leaving him howling in agony among some of Reenie's prized roses towards the rear of the garden. The thorns had also ripped at his skin as he'd tried to stand up and so he'd laid there shivering and bleeding for what seemed the best part of the night before Gertie had come to his rescue. Reenie had laughed like a drain at his predicament while she helped get him to his feet and cleaned him up enough to move him comfortably to the temporary hospital, he'd been lying there most of the day after being swabbed and bandaged after he was admitted to the ward, the suit that he had been wearing was now in tatters hanging over the back of a nearby chair. Reenie hadn't said anything, but he knew she'd be looking to him to replace the suit, but at that time he was too ill to worry about the repercussions so as he lay there moaning to himself. Gertie looked on at him as she clicked away with her knitting needles and a ball of some oddly coloured yarn, she peered over a small pair of horn-rimmed glasses.

"You can count yourself lucky," she said to him with a wry smile on her face.

Alby didn't need to think too long about his answer. He sharply replied, telling her that it was alright being wise after the event, but how the hell could he possibly count himself lucky as a dog had just taken liberties with his backside. They both sat in silence again with the only sound coming from the

149

nurse's shoes clipping along the stone floor merging into the click-clack of Gertie's knitting needles churning out another one of her grossly inaccurate versions of a cable knit sweater, her speciality since her granny had shown her how to knit when she was a young girl to while away the hours when it became too cold to play outside. Gertie looked over the top of her string of wool and scorned Alby that he had ruined those trousers, Reenie would never forgive him. Alby lifted his chin off the battered pillow and looked across at the ruined suit stained with his blood, feeling even more sorry for himself he told her that Reenie could 'clear off' he should have 'just peed in them' and then he wouldn't be in that situation 'would he!'

"Still you are lucky, Alby," Gertie replied, without looking up from her knitting.

A short time passed and neither spoke, it was just before three in the afternoon and Alby had been thinking about their last altercation.

"Gertie?" Alby enquired in a soft delicate tone, which he'd devised down the years to get her full attention and his point across in a way that would stop her sniping. "Earlier this week, Jerry drops a bomb on my gaff and leaves me without a stitch to wear and last night, Reenie's flaming next door neighbour's dog takes a chunk out of my bum and with it half a yard of Uncle George's best Harris tweed and all you can say is," raising his tone for impact, "'still you are lucky Alby'." A rueful smile creased Gertie's lips as she explained that, if the dog hadn't bitten his bottom and dragged him through the roses, he would have been smack in the middle of a bomb crater when they found him this morning, and he would have been considerably slimmer than he'd started out.

This made Alby think and so again they sat in stony

silence until Alby could bear it no longer.

"How big is it then?" he asked, nodding his head back towards his bandaged backside.

"The bomb crater?" she joked.

"No the hole in my…"

"Alby!" Gertie leapt in before Alby could finish his sentence and before any of the other patients could hear his foul mouth.

"I tell you we should have gone down the tube with all the others," she told him. Alby clenched his fists and banged them several times on his pillow in frustration.

"You're flaming priceless," he said, Gertie just carried on dropping stitches in her cable knit.

Along the corridor Nurse Beth was just starting her duty, she'd been attached to the hospital since she had trained back in the twenties, it had already been a very long start to her day and she'd heard every excuse and every cry of pain whether they were genuine or not, she'd become an expert in sorting the wheat from the chaff and Alby was the next patient for her to check on. Checking her notes, she's already found out what the others had written about him from earlier in the day, so she was in no mood to be messed around by a patient with what they described as a 'small flesh wound by a dog to posterior' with the patient being described as rotund, old, and grumpy and in general need of a wash and some clean clothes.

As she entered her makeshift ward the other much younger nurses who had been on duty for some time were heard to scurry about from bed to bed arranging corners and linen as if their lives depended on it, Nurse Beth was old school and expected her team to behave in a manner that was becoming of such an environment, she wasn't at all happy with the fresh new faces bringing in their new ways in such austere times and she expected her patients to behave in a similar manner, she was in charge and what she said went, although she wasn't adverse to the odd joke at a patients expense, especially those types of patient that fell into Alby's bracket. 'Old and grumpy,' Alby was to be her next challenge of the day and as she approached his bed with a stern studious look on her face. Alby looked up from the pillow he'd been biting and called out in a rather woeful manner as if to try to show her how much pain he was in, "I say, nurse, how long am I going to be like this?"

The nurse picked up Alby's notes that were hanging by an old clip from the end of his wrought iron hospital bed and without looking in Alby's direction she tersely answered, "How long is a piece of string young man?"

Gertie couldn't contain herself and chortled loudly to herself as Alby huffed into the pillow, "You're as bad as she is." Alby flicked his head towards where Gertie was sitting, still laughing, and still trying to pick up the stitches she'd dropped earlier in the row now occupying her old needles. "What's the matter with all you people?" Alby generalised. Gertie said nothing and no answer came from the old nurse, Alby went on to tell them that they needed something to liven the place up, Gertie sighed she knew exactly where this was going she'd seen it many times in the pub on a Sunday afternoon when it had been on the quiet side, Alby proceeded to sing, very badly, 'if you were the only girl in the world' singing to the nurse, she let him get a few lines into his song and just about into the flow, when, slowly she raised her index figure and placed it across her lips, Alby chose to ignore her and carried on.

"You can be noisy, or you can be quiet, but all you have is a small little scratch on your backside and you are making more fuss than all our expectant mothers down the corridor." "Now," she continued, "I suggest you grow up or I'll get Matron and when she hears about you." Alby thought about that for a brief moment, and then he quickly let the nurse know that there really wasn't any need for her to do that. Fetching a thermometer from a cup by the side of his bed she thrust it firmly into Alby's mouth and as she did so she muttered to herself that hopefully, it would keep him quiet for a while.

Turning to Gertie, she asked if he was always such a bad patient. "He always has something to say," Gertie replied.

After several minutes of squirming on the bed trying to get comfortable, the nurse asked Alby to turn over so that she could attend his wound. Alby had moved himself into an odd position on the bed whilst still sucking on the large glass thermometer, the nurse somehow managed to get the gauge from Alby's mouth but his fidgeting meant that his backside was now almost covered with blankets and as he lay back and looked up at the swirling fans, whirling rhythmically on the ceiling, the nurse posed Alby a question. "Well, you have a choice," she said as she shrugged her shoulders at Alby. "I clean the wound and redress it or I don't clean the wound and redress it."

At this point, the nurse stopped what she was doing, Alby hadn't spoken or moved an inch since she'd asked him to, so for effect the nurse told Alby that gangrene would then set in and drinking wouldn't be the only thing he'd have to do through a straw. "Do you understand!" she shouted. Alby stayed silent. The nurse hand one last move, one last trick that she had always used on the very obstinate patients that passed through her wards. "Well," she said, "do you want matron to come and talk to you?" It always worked. Nobody wanted being scalded by the offhand nature of the ward matron, not even the hospital doctors liked facing their wrath, even if they were in the right, which more often than not they were.

Alby didn't need to think a moment longer. "No, no, no. Of course not!" he blurted out quickly. "Whatever you say, I'll turn over then…yeah, OK!"

Gertie quickly put her knitting down in a pile without even making sure she hadn't dropped any of her precious stitches, she'd become frustrated by Alby's behaviour and thought he was showing them both up. Standing up, she approached the bed from Alby's blindside and quickly hissed into his available ear to stop acting like a big kid. When Gertie finished berating Alby, the nurse told her that she would show her how the dressing should be applied so that they could get him cleaned up again and out of the hospital as they needed the beds for more, 'pressing complaints.' Alby's injuries, whilst horrific, were, minor by comparison to some that had been ferried into the makeshift hospital overnight from bomb sites all over the capital.

As the nurse gently but firmly tugged on the swaths of bandages that had been used to dress his wounds earlier, she started to reveal the extent of Alby's injuries in the cold light of the day. Gertie winced at the sight of the crusty, stale, blood-stained mish-mash of his damaged backside. "Oh that's nasty, isn't it?" she said, almost hiding behind her hands and peering through her fingers as she said it.

"Very nasty," the nurse said coldly. "Lucky to still have something to sit on," she added with a smile, whilst ignoring

Alby's pleas for painkillers and sympathy.

"That would have been a shame," Gertie said, "as he does a lot of that!"

"Not very active then?" asked the nurse.

"Not very." Gertie was enjoying poking fun at her man's demise; she watched as the nurse carried on cleaning Alby up and smiled with a wince as the nurse covered the wound in some fresh iodine. Alby howled like a lame dog, obviously in pain, as the brown, yellowish, orange coloured liquid ran randomly all over his backside and down the tops of his legs as the nurse tried her best to disinfect the wound, which had been torn apart by the dog, with a huge swab of cotton wool that had been dipped in the ointment. Alby gave an anguished cry as it touched the raw flesh but the nurse remained unmoved by his squeamishness and once she was certain the wound was clean and that there was no debris left there to infect his body further, she wrapped it in several cotton pads and a number of bandages. All the time instructing Gertie how to wrap the wound so that it would not fall off and become dirty, should Alby move around in a more athletic manner at some point later that day or week!

When the nurse finished, she peered at Alby and gave him a rather disdainful look.

"Would you like to sit down?" she said matter-of-factly.

"What?" said Alby.

"Sit down!" she instructed, curtly. Alby tried his best to slowly turn and put his somewhat oversized backside down on the bed but as he did so the pain of his wounds was sheer agony and the big fellow let out a piercing cry. Each time he moved, it was the same. Every time his weighty backside came into contact with the bed, the pain was excruciating and fearful of creating more pain than he could face, he just could not bring himself to lower his rear end down and so now stranded like an upside-down spider spread-eagled across the bed with Gertie laughing uncontrollably and the nurse becoming more and more frustrated. Alby was faced with a simple fact, 'he had no choice'. So, limply, he rolled and collapsed into a heap on his side across the bed.

"Oh crickey love!" he exclaimed. "I can't do it. It makes me Harris twitch, can't I just lay here a bit longer?" he asked both, in a very infantile manner. Immediately, the nurse brought her hand down sharply and slapped Alby across his backside.

"No!" she said tersely. "We need to get you up." In the instant that her hand connected with Alby's bare flesh, his cries could have been heard south of the water. It took him a full minute to regain any kind of composure, still he was reluctant to move from where he was lying, prone, half on his side, half on his back on the old iron bed. As the nurse continued to wait, she became increasingly impatient, resisting the temptation to give Alby's backside another slap, she grabbed him by his shirt sleeves and tried to pull him to his feet.

"Come on then," she said, "what's keeping you?" Alby gingerly started to rise from the bed, the look of disgust on his face said enough, the nurse had seen it all before and wasn't in the least bit daunted by Alby's continued pain-wracked cries and quick-witted observations. As Alby eventually got to his feet, he took a long look at the nurse who had by now stood some way back from the bed, arms folded as she in turn, looked on at Alby's wretched movements.

"I don't know who's worse," Alby spoke, in a whisper too

himself, "you or bleeding Hitler."

Standing himself upright as best he could he gathered his thoughts and he looked at Gertie.

"Let's get out of here," he said, "before she does me any more damage." Gertie turned and moved towards her man taking his weight under his arm Gertie shuffled towards the doorway.

As the pair reached the exit the nurse took Alby's torn trousers from the back of the chair where they had been put earlier, running her fingers up and down the rips and snags of the old material she smiled to herself as she called after Alby and Gertie, "Will you not be wanting these?" Gertie smiled.

"Not unless you're an expert in invisible mending," she said, disappearing through the exit and out into the dust and gloom of London's late summer afternoon.

***

Ralph and Four Eyes led everyone down the rails towards tunnel three and as they entered the murky darkness of the underground system, the smell of exploded cordite was rich in the air making everyone start to cough and splutter as it entered their lungs, the ladies were finding the going tough in their heels but the thought of the children possibly being buried alive spurred them all on.

Ralph carried on relentlessly towards where he thought the explosion took place, as torch beams bounced off the arching ceilings of the tunnels, every now and again a stray London animal would be catapulted into the spotlight as a frenzy of bodies scared them into the higher perches along the route. Rats mingled at foot level, their high-pitched squeals becoming more and more evident as the swarms of rodents were backed further into the tunnels. Coming to a junction in the rail system, Ralph stopped suddenly and urged the assembled crowd to be silent. He shone his torch briefly up all the tunnels in front of them. There were two on the left and three more to the right of them and Ralph had to make sure he chose the right tunnel otherwise they would disappear into the network and pass right by where they should be at a different level. Still, the smell of spent arms hung heavily in the air but the only sounds that could be heard were the distant trains and the animals that called the area, home.

Ralph picked the third tunnel to the right and gestured to all that they should follow him. They moved off quickly in the direction Ralph was telling them to, but literally just as they all got into the tunnel, they were suddenly backed up against a huge pile of debris.

The dust had settled all around and as people flashed the available torch beams up and over the huge stack in front of them; the horror of what had happened suddenly became evident. A vast area of the tunnel section had collapsed large concrete and iron beams lay in a tangled mess. The brickwork that had once formed the magnificent archways of the underground tunnels was lying in complete disarray. Water from bent and broken underground pipes were seeping through the pile at all levels and forming huge dirty black pools around their feet, but still, there was no sound. "My word, this is a mess," Ralph said, the panic was evident in his voice. "We need some more light down here. Can everyone who has a torch come to the front?" About four people rushed forward and shone their small lights at the stack as they all waited for Ralph to decide what was the best course of action that they should all take.

Ralph slowly removed his trilby hat and wiped a bead of sweat that had started to run, from his brow, before placing the hat back at a deliberately jaunty angle. Reaching into his suit jacket, he pulled out a packet of Capstan full strength. Slowly, he took a cigarette from the packet and placed it with finesse into the left-hand side of his mouth. He struck a match from the book he had held within the back pocket of his trousers, a compartment he never used for customer stock. Taking a long first draw on his cigarette, he then let the smoke slowly drift from his mouth and nose. As the smoke burnt into one of his eyes, he squinted before rubbing at the eye roughly to stop it stinging. Ralph mulled over his next decision as two of the older men at the back shouted that nothing was being done and that they should all do something urgently. They rushed forward towards the stack, but Ralph, nonchalantly held up his right arm, he said nothing, the two men immediately stopped in their tracks. Reenie then turned and faced the crowd.

"Don't touch anything till my Gerald gets down here," she said, trying to take some sort of control.

"We can't wait for the rozzers to get down here. If anyone's trapped, they'll never get out alive," one of the old men said angrily. Suddenly, Charlie, who hadn't said a thing since they'd climbed down into the tunnels, grabbed at some of the bricks that lay scattered at his feet and threw them back along the tunnel in anger.

"I thought all these places had been blocked off. Nobody should have been down here anyway," he said hurling a rusty piece of old iron aside.

Ralph who had continued to draw on his cigarette spoke

in a quiet, more thoughtful tone, "How can you block off an entire rail network? Use your loaf son." Taking a last draw on his cigarette, he stubbed it out under his once perfectly polished brogues. He held his finger to his lips and called for hush as he then called out towards the stack.

"Hello, can anyone hear us? Hello….hello….Nothing, not a sound, did anyone hear anything?"

They could all see into the disused tunnel over the very top of the pile but none of them could get through any of the tiny gaps that were left by all the fallen debris, Charlie looked at Four Eyes who was still silently crying to herself and he asked if she was 'really' sure, that, that is where they should be looking. She nodded and tearfully told them all that she was the only one to get out. At this point, many of the others started to slowly pick up bricks from the pile and throw them further back down the tunnel from where they came. Charlie and the others started to join in. Forming a chain they started to pass the debris back from person to person and stack it all clear of where they were standing. They did this for five minutes but it was clear the task unfolding was more than they alone could manage. Charlie stopped what he was doing and looked at Ralph.

"We can't just tear at it with our bare hands and hope to find something." The frustration of the task was affecting more than just Charlie. Reenie, too, stopped and sat down on a pile of bricks that had been stacked by where she was in the chain.

"I bet you know the tunnels like the back of your hands, Ralph. Can't you think of something?" Ralph scratched at his chin as he thought of what Reenie had just said.

"Let me think," he said before calling Four Eyes over. She

scurried over to Ralph and he bent over to speak to her. Taking his handkerchief from his jacket pocket, he gently wiped a dusty tear that had welled up in the corner of her eye. Ralph had an option, and he needed the little girl to help. As he explained to her that she was their only option, a sparkle started to return to her face. She realised she was important in what Ralph needed. He told the girl to go with one of the ladies and to go up the stairway which he had shown them previously. When they get outside, she, with the lady, were to round up all the help they could muster and then come back into the doorway but instead of going down the stairway to the right like they had previously, she should go left for about twenty-five yards and then take the stairs there, which if his thinking was correct would bring them out on the other side of this mess, as he finished talking to her she was already taking the hand of a tall blonde lady who was standing in the group of people piling bricks.

"Go on, what you waiting for?" urged Ralph as the pair raced off down the line towards the stairway. As they watched them disappear, Ralph addressed the others, "Me and Charlie will drop through that hatch over there. It should bring us out, at the other end over there," pointing beyond the huge pile of rubble. "By coming back on ourselves, we might just be able to find the kids and save them." Charlie shook his head and pursed his weathered lips.

"I'm not sure about this mate," he said, backing away slightly from the group. Connie took hold of his arm and placed her head on his shoulder in a loving manner.

"Go on, Charlie. Remember what we talked about?" Embarrassed, Charlie coyly pushed Connie's head to the side and moved towards Ralph, who was now standing by the big iron hatchway that was in the tunnel wall about three feet from the floor.

The hatchway itself looked incredibly heavy and was covered in rust. The bolts holding it shut hadn't been moved for years but as Ralph clouted them in turn with a large piece of concrete, they broke free from the scaly rust, enabling the door to swing open. Charlie peered into the gloom behind the hatch, crossed himself and looked at Ralph. "OK mate," he said, "you lead the way." And as Ralph lifted himself into the small hatchway, Connie ran forward towards Charlie.

"Give us a blooming kiss," she said pursing her lips as she covered the ground between herself and the jaunty cockney. Charlie looked at his feet, like it was if he was a child again being asked to give his granny a goodbye hug. His hands were in his pockets and he bit at his bottom lip, looking over at Winnie she just shrugged her giant shoulders and raised an eyebrow. Connie launched herself at Charlie and grabbing his cheeks with her hands, she planted a long lingering kiss and then as she pulled back and looked deep into his eyes, he too climbed into the hatchway and disappeared after Ralph.

Once inside the shaft, Charlie immediately became claustrophobic. It was only about three feet wide and was in complete darkness. Once having been used as a service shaft many years previously when the tunnels were built, it had laid dormant until Ralph and Charlie had clambered into it. Charlie shuffled along painfully on his knees as the old brickwork cut deep into his skin, Ralph called back to him making sure he was still there as he pressed keenly on ahead. Now and again something sharp on the floor of the shaft would pierce one of their knees and they would yelp out in pain caused by the unseen assailant.

They crawled along for about 300 hundred yards, occasionally, they would stop to rest up, sitting with their backs to the wall. Their eyes had become adjusted to the lack of light but still, it was almost totally black in the service shaft. It took almost half an hour for them to emerge from the shaft at the point where Ralph thought they could double back towards the trapped children and as they clambered out into the disused tunnel again. They were hit by the blanket of spent cordite that was hanging heavy in the tube's atmosphere.

Ralph checked his pockets to make sure he hadn't dropped anything in the shaft and then dusted himself down, ever the immaculately dressed man, he was now though, somewhat ragged with his trousers all torn and stained with the dirt and oil from crawling along the shaft. He readjusted his trilby hat once more and set off in the direction of the disused platform with Charlie not far behind him.

Charlie took an unfortunate tumble. *More pain*, he thought. *This caring lark was starting to wear thin,* he thought to himself as he picked himself up from the floor of the tunnel.

As they entered the old disused platform, the extent of the damage was clear at the far end the tube was blocked as it had been from the other side, but Ralph was drawn to an area about halfway along where the damage was not so great. A wall had caved in but the ceiling which had formed part of the arch was still intact. He'd remembered that many of the artefacts that he shown the children had been in this area and he hoped that they had been congregating there when the explosion happened. The platform itself was in an absolute mess all the crates and their secret contents had been blown about and most of the beautiful ceramic green-and-cream tiles that lined the station had been dislodged from the walls.

Ralph got to the area where the wall had caved in, and in the murk found a pile of debris all propped up by large iron girders lying across one another with all kinds of broken brick and concrete structure propped against these. Ralph stopped and called out to the children.

Winnie, Reenie along with Connie and Alice had stayed in the tunnel at the other end in case they had got into trouble in the tiny shaft but they could hear both Ralph and Charlie in the other tunnel beyond the mass of tangled iron and brick, hauling lumps of concrete aside in their quest to find the missing gang. Ralph continued to call out to the children while throwing more and more debris from the collapsed wall aside. Suddenly, a small, almost unidentifiable noise came from inside the pile, Ralph thinking it may have been one of the children's small voices, raced to the spot where he thought it came from.

"Quick, Charlie boy, over here." Charlie immediately stopped dragging more and more off the main pile and raced over to where Ralph was.

"Here's one of the little bleeders, give us a hand." Ralph had sunk to his knees and removed some large pieces of concrete to reveal what looked like a small aperture in the pile of broken wall. As he reached in, he had felt the arm of one of the missing children, cold to the touch and covered in brick dust but almost certainly alive and well. Ralph steadied himself before managing to gently but surely pull the first child clear of the stack. Charlie immediately took the grubby boy from Ralph's grasp and sat him down on the old platforms edge, briefly, he checked him over to make sure he was going to be alright as he did so.

Connie had climbed to the top of the stack at the other side and was eagerly trying to hear what Ralph and Charlie were doing on their side of the blockage.

"I think they've found one!" she shouted to the others on her side, getting herself into a better position on the pile so that she could try and converse with Ralph and Charlie. She shouted over the top of the stack, hoping for some news to filter across to them on their side.

"I say," she shouted, "is the child, OK?" Her question was met with an eerie silence, she slapped her sides in frustration.

"They can't hear it's too far away," she called back to the others who were by now sitting on the old stacks of bricks which they had all started to pile up before Ralph and Charlie had disappeared into the small shaft. Stepping down off the large piece of broken concrete, she had perched on to try and look over the stack, Connie slowly walked back towards the other girls.

Reenie was sitting back from the main group of ladies after they had all made it clear how they felt regarding her association with Ralph.

Determined to show he wasn't all bad, Reenie muttered, almost to herself, as she kicked at a pile of concrete dust. "You might all dislike that spiv, but if it wasn't for him, it looks like those children may never have got out alive."

Winnie had never liked the spiv since she'd encountered him the very first time she'd ventured into the station at Aldwych. He'd caught her eye and offered her some fragrant soap and then went on to tell her it would knock years off her, much to Charlie's amusement and her annoyance.

"And if it wasn't for him, they may never have been up this part of the tunnel in the first place!" she sneered at Renee's comment raising her voice. As she did so, sending some of the rats that had settled back into their usual routines scurrying off in all directions.

"Oh don't be so stupid," Connie snapped back. "These children have been running around with gay abandon ever since we came down the tube." Winnie's look said everything she felt about Connie's last comment, and she turned her back on the socialite. Connie carried on telling them that there had been little or no discipline from the children and that you could hardly blame their failings on the spiv as they'd probably all just 'tagged along anyway'.

Reenie suddenly stood up from the pile that she'd been sitting on and ferociously turned on Winnie, pointing her finger towards where Ralph was on the other side of the mess, she angrily tore Winnie off a strip, as she told her that they could all do so with his spirit, as nothing seems to deter him.

She finished her tirade and turned back towards the stack of debris, raising herself up on her tiptoes as if to look over the huge pile, she called out to Ralph on the other side, "Are you ok Ralph, do you need a hand?" She was oblivious to everyone's knowing look at each other; Winnie was aghast and shaking her head she muttered to herself about Reenie's reputation being in tatters, as a broad smile started to grow across her stubbled chin. Some good things can come out of a tragedy she thought to herself.

On the other side, Ralph and Charlie had been beavering away at the collapsed structure which entombed the children. His first chance to stop, Ralph stood and arched his back, desperately trying to rid his body of the aches and pains he was feeling from all the hard work. Shouting back, he told the women that most of the children had been found safe and well but that they weren't going to move them until help arrived from above. It went silent again from that side of the stack, all the girls looked at each other. Reenie broke the silence as she shouted back and told Ralph to look after himself, Winnie's ears pricked at the sound of Reenie gushing towards the big man at the others expense.

In the old station, Charlie picked up on Reenie's feelings as she'd called out to Ralph, he smiled to himself.

"I'd say you got an admirer there, son," he said to Ralph as they sat the next child down on the station edge after they had pulled her from the pile of broken concrete. Ralph, by now, had removed his jacket and stowed it safely and neatly folded on the one clean crate he could find, making sure his 'stock' was still safely tucked away in their given compartments. He pushed his trilby further up his forehead, the Capstan full strength he'd been drawing on was about to relinquish a long dark snake of ash as it balanced delicately on the tip of his cigarette. He stood, his big hands digging deeply into the base of his spine, as he stretched backwards to try and ease his tiring muscles, he looked at Charlie and told him they didn't have time for that kind of rubbish as they hadn't accounted for all the kids.

"I'm sure there should be one more," he said.

Charlie looked around at the children they had lined up along the platforms edge. Slowly, he counted them to himself, there seemed to be a lot of children, but it was dark and they were covered from head to foot in dust and dirt. Their little faces blackened and hair all matted together. He didn't really recognise any of them but he knew them, he must have known, they were all Four Eyes' mates.

"How do you know?" mystified, he scratched at his head as he asked Ralph.

"Cause Josey ain't here and he's the kids' leader." A sudden chill came over Charlie, the hairs on the back of his neck peered out over the top of his collar. Taking Ralph by his arm, he urged, begged, they had to find him.

"That's Winnie's boy. We got to find him!" Ralph looked at the line of children.

"Where's Josey. Was he with you lot when this all collapsed?" Hastily Ralph went up and down the line of children asking each in turn if they knew of Josey's whereabouts. Slimey pointed to the pile of twisted girders and ironwork.

"He's under that lot I think, but I haven't heard a sound from him in a while," he said hesitantly.

Winnie and the other ladies hadn't heard anything from the opposite side of the stack for almost five minutes and by now, they were all pacing up and down in the darkened passages way of the underground network. Occasionally, they would stub their shoes on a brick or piece of concrete. Connie's beautiful dark suede boots were now scraped and scratched beyond repair; she likened them to a pair of dirty old work boots.

Winnie had been very quiet since her last outburst, keeping herself to herself and not wanting to engage in a conversation with any of them. She'd stopped pacing and had sat back down.

"If Josey's with that lot, I'll tan his backside, so help me." She suddenly opened up again. "Charlie!" she raised her voice in the direction of where the rescue was taking place. Speculatively, she threw out another question in their direction, "Charlie! Is Josey down there?" Josey never did spend much time with them these days and so she never really knew where he was apart from the evenings he'd slept with them all in the tubes.

"I don't know, love!" Charlie shouted back from the other end.

"What do you mean, I don't know? Either is or he isn't. What is it?" Winnie was now getting frustrated.

"Can you all be quiet!" Ralph needed to think and the voices echoing around the tunnels was distracting him. "There's still one unaccounted for," he called back. Deliberately, he didn't say Josey's name so not to upset Winnie. The girls, though immediately, all turned to her, assuring her, that there must be a reason why Josey was not among those found. Winnie, however, tried to seem unconcerned at the boy's fate. she was sure he was still on the outside playing 'as boys do'.

Ralph urgently looked around the platform, kicking over crates and under piles of blankets, he found a long length of strong rope and dashed back to the stack. "Look Charlie," he said, "I think I can get myself under that lot and have a good poke around. Tie this rope around me, you can then pull me clear if things turn nasty."

"You're mad!" exclaimed Charlie, barely believing that Ralph would risk such a thing. Charlie started to tie the rope in a clove hitch around Ralphs's waist.

"If it wasn't for me, they wouldn't have known about this place would they?" Ralph felt responsible for the predicament that the children were in. Charlie finished the knot and gave it a quick tug pulling Ralph towards him as he did so.

"You sure about this?" he said, but Ralph was already on his hands and knees, clearing an even bigger passageway into the pile of fallen masonry so his large frame could fit into the gap.

With no news forthcoming from the old station where the children were being rescued, the ladies had become irritated by the lack of communication coming their way.

"What's that spiv up to now?" Winnie shouted, without getting up from her perch among the piles of fallen brickwork. Charlie heard her voice on his side, but didn't answer, he was concentrating on Ralph and the other girls had said very little to her since her previous outburst. "Rooting around for more ill-gotten gains no doubt," she said, to herself, although, loud enough for Charlie on the other side of the pile to pick up on.

Charlie, still annoyed by her previous outburst, called back, and told her that Ralph was looking for Josey, so she should "Keep her north and south shut as Ralph might just do you a turn."

Winnie was now concerned for Josey's welfare. Previously, she'd thought that he was far away, playing with others not down in the dirty old tunnels when the explosion had occurred.

"What do you mean he's looking for Josey? Ain't you found all the kids safe and well then?" There was now an undeniable sense of terror in Winnie's voice and Charlie needed her to remain calm.

"All except Josey. Now pipe down will you and listen and where's the blinkin help from above?"

Charlie was becoming anxious as they had all the children with them, with various injuries, they couldn't look after them all and they were also still looking for Josey. Winnie was in a desperate state, her boy was under the pile and they hadn't located him, she ran over to the stack climbed to the top and peering through the gap as best she could she called out, "I'm sure it's coming Charlie, but please for god's sake make sure my boys safe." Charlie looked up at the tiny hole that was still left in the tunnel where the main structure had collapsed and could just about see Winnie's desperate face through the gloom. "You better start praying that Ralph here is going to help."

Suddenly, further along the platform, Four Eyes burst onto the old station as she led an eager mass of helpers through the devastation caused by the explosion. They picked their way carefully desperate not to disturb anything that might cause another fall from the ageing brickwork, most of them were all carrying torches and the tunnel illuminated eerily, as the shadows from the lights danced around the tiled brickwork. They immediately got to work on the rescued children, cleaning and tending their wounds applying bandages and gently carrying them back the way they had come up the old staircase to the surface and some clean air, to be given further treatment by nurses who had rushed over from the Charing Cross Hospital.

Under the stack laying on his stomach, Ralph was inching his way towards where he thought Josey was caught, gingerly he moved lumps of concrete and broken bricks from his path until fishing in his trouser pockets. Ralph found a small paper book of matches most of which hadn't been struck, using one of these matches to illuminate his way forward, he caught sight of Josey, the boy looked in a bad way his right leg had been forced backwards and was bent at an uncharacteristic angle, Josey's eyes were also tightly closed as if he was in severe pain, Ralph feared the worse, gently he called the boy's name then paused for a second or two, there was no response, calling again Josey's eyes flickered into life, wide and pain-wracked, Ralph assured the boy that he was going to be safe and that he would get him out, quickly he looked him over checking the extent of the boy's injuries and then called back to Charlie.

"Charlie I'm with the boy, it looks like he's broken his leg quite badly and it's trapped under some sort of old metal girder. If I can just move this bleedin thing out the way I might just be able to squeeze his leg out." As Ralph fumbled about in the dark trying his best to dislodge what had trapped Josey's leg, the rubble started to shift uneasily around the two of them.

"I've done it but the boys in a bad way, get some help here fast." Three of the men who had come to their aid rushed forward but Charlie urged them to wait until they were sure it was safe, and Josey and Ralph were clear of the stack before any more rubble was removed.

"If you put the rope around the boy, I can pull him clear," Charlie called out impatiently tapping his fingers on the pile as he waited for Ralphs next move.

Eventually, Ralph answered from inside the mass of collapsed tunnel wall, "OK Charlie but be careful. We don't want this lot coming down on me or him. OK, I've tied the rope, start pulling."

Charlie and the men started to gradually pull at the rope, slowly at first until they were sure everything was going to be alright and no further tunnelling was about to collapse and on Ralphs advice, they gave the rope one last gentle tug, Josey appeared from under the stack. The boy was in a really bad way, crying out in pain. His clothes were torn from his upper body, revealing an enormous number of cuts and tears to his young skin. His face was also blackened by the soot and dust caused by the explosion that ripped the tunnel apart. They quickly untied the rope which Ralph had threaded through the boy's belt loops on his tatty grey flannel trousers and laid him back down on a pile of dusty blankets that the men had made into a makeshift bed, calling urgently for a doctor. Charlie got down as close to Josey as he could, to talk to him, and told him how they had managed to get everyone out safe and well apart from a few cuts and bruises, Josey appeared to smile.

Ralph himself suddenly reappeared from out of the stack emerging backwards, he dusted himself off and refitted his trilby hat at its correct angle before lighting another capstan cigarette. He sat back and took a long-deserved puff on the dry tobacco, he winked at Charlie as he did so.

"A job well done. That was close. Lords knows what we would have done if he'd been trapped any worse," said Ralph as he emitted a gentle stream of cigarette smoke out through his long thin nose. Charlie got up from where he had been tending to Josey and crossed his legs as he sat down on the dirty platform not even attempting to make the area clean before he sat down. "Lord knows what we would have done without you," Charlie told him patting the genial giant on his shoulder.

Connie's voice suddenly broke through all the commotion as the doctors and nurses who had attended to Josey's broken leg carried the stricken lad out on a stretcher. She'd managed to get her small frame to the top of the pile and was now peering through the small gap making sure her neatly coiffured hair didn't touch the soot encrusted underground ceiling. She asked Charlie what was happening and whether Josey had been rescued safe and well.

"Of course, we have!" Charlie shouted back he too was

now drawing on one of Ralphs cigarettes taking a much-earned break from their escapades. "Without Ralph here though, we'd have been scuppered. He deserves a blooming medal. He does." Reenie's face appeared alongside Connie's and she called out to Ralph making sure that he was OK.

"'course, I am, girl," the unflappable spiv nonchalantly called back towards where the tiny face appeared in the gloom. Taking the last puff on his cigarette, he stood up and discarded the tiny butt. Grabbing at Charlie's arm, he helped Charlie get to his feet. They both stood there for a second and surveyed the devastation once more. Ralph called to the girls to get back to the station and urged the men around them that they needed to get the damage shored up as soon as possible.

Teams of men had already started to sift through the wreckage and stack bricks and concrete in various piles along the length of the old station, others were working to move the large beams of iron that had supported the tunnel's wall before it collapsed, soon the tunnel was a hive of activity as everyone set to work making the tunnel a safe place once again. Charlie watched them all working, his muscles tired from all they had done to help the children, but, in the corner of his eye, something stood out, something that he believed they should have and use to good effect. He tapped Ralph on the shoulder and pointing away off to the far end of the tunnel, he showed Ralph.

"Look, there's an old Joanna over there. Let's get a load of these guys to help us take it back to the station. We could have a blinkin good old knees up later on." Ralph smiled.

"And you can leave the tap water to me, Charlie boy. We'll celebrate in style."

They both chuckled away to themselves proud of what

they had achieved together.

Gerald was, by now, assigning people jobs; men were to help out in the tunnel shoring up and the ladies were to help make cups of tea for the men and medical teams. All of the children had, by now, been transferred by London Taxis to the hospital at Charing cross and a team of medics were on standby in case any further collapses occurred. Gerald came down the steps and entered the scene of his downfall and remembered how he had nearly managed to catch his prized villain the previous night. Anger boiled within him, it now appeared that not only had he lost his treasured wife to the spiv but that Ralph was also now a public hero. He was never going to live it down back at the station, his inspector would encourage others and his life would be made hell. He needed to come out of it on top but nothing had gone his way at all over the previous twenty-four hours what could he do. He stood there briefly, alone in his thoughts. Off to his right, coming from behind the piano that Charlie had spotted some minutes earlier a spluttering sound could be heard. He shook his head, all the children had been accounted for no one else had been in the tunnel when it collapsed. He passed it off as rats making noises but as it grew, he stepped down off of the platform and onto the track. As he neared the piano, Ardle suddenly stood up, the pain had subsided and he had awoken after collapsing in a heap following the explosion. As he saw the policeman, he rubbed his eyes and tried to adjust his vision, pinching himself to make sure he wasn't dreaming. He again rubbed his eyes. Gerald stood stock still and beamed at the luckless Irish man standing behind the treasured piano in the darkness. Ardle reached down to his left and as he grabbed Paddy's collar, he pulled Paddy up to his feet. Gerald couldn't believe his luck, it seemed to be changing. He looked upwards and said a small prayer under his breath.

***

"We should have blinkin well gone down the tube in the first place." Alby was on a roll; they'd arrived back at Reenie's house from the hospital earlier that day and he'd had a good sleep. They were in Reenie's back parlour a small little annexe to the rear of her quaint little terrace. Pictures of her garden and the odd picture of her wedding day to Gerald hung from brass hooks hammered badly into the walls. The walls themselves were covered in a dowdy brown mud colour. The only vivid injection of colour coming from the small curtains Reenie had made herself that were hanging at the small rear window that now looked out onto the devastation of the previous evening. But now, after a hot sweet cup of tea, he was back to his usual self, bellowing at Gertie. Everything was wrong. The seat was too high or too hard. He couldn't get comfortable and if the bed was downstairs, it would be easier. He sat there frowning to himself.

"If we'd gone down the tube in the first place, none of this would have happened," he told Gertie as he took another sip from a new cup of tea Gertie had just made him. He winced as the hot drink scalded the back of his throat, Gertie was sat at the table desperately trying to make good the errors she had made to her knitting whilst sitting with Alby in the hospital and was unconcerned at his troubles. Her glasses were perched on the end of her very Jewish nose with her hair pulled back in a tight bun and hid under a small black net. The lines in her face belied her age; years of caring for the cantankerous old man had left her battle scarred although her love for the person she had wed all those years ago was unquestioned. She couldn't help feeling his version of events fell short of what actually had occurred.

"We would still have been bombed, Alby."

"I know," he said. "But I would still have had me own clothes, wouldn't I and then if I'd have wanted to take a pee in them, I could have, couldn't I? Then I wouldn't have a scene from the Bayeux tapestry on me Harris would I?" His sarcastic tones did little to shake Gertie out of her concentration.

"No, Alby, you wouldn't," was all she could offer in defence. Alby moved gingerly to his right-leaning over a pile of clothes that had just been washed by some of their old neighbours who'd saved them from their bombed-out home. He switched on the radio to hear what the home office would be broadcasting, turning the dial in both directions he heard nothing apart from the familiar crackle of a radio without reception. He then turned the big brown switch on the radio's side to the off position. They sat there in stony silence; Gertie intent on clicking away with her needles and Alby slowly sipping his rapidly cooling cup of tea. As the minutes dragged by, Gertie would occasionally look up and smile at Alby but it was met with no reaction from him whatsoever.

"I've lost everything in this blinkin war," he said. "Me home, me dignity. I can't remember when I last had a good night's sleep. If Jerry comes over here, I'll make sure I send 'em back without a stitch on." Alby had suddenly cut through the silence which made Gertie drop another stitch. Slamming her work down on the table, she removed her glasses and walked across the room to where Alby was sitting.

"Oh Alby! Give it a rest, will you!" she shouted at him shaking her head. Standing there with her hands on her hips, she looked a formidable opponent. Alby shrunk back into the chair and offered nothing in return. "I'm tired of hearing how this war has affected you. What about the rest of us?" She paused, waiting for Alby to speak but he knew better and decided to bite his lip. Instead, he kept his eyes firmly on the worn-out linoleum that kept the cold at bay in the old parlour room. "None of us has slept easy for months; none of us has eaten a proper meal in months." She was on a roll and the effect it had had on Alby was clear. His stern face had disappeared and been replaced by a little boy who had been caught with his hand in the biscuit jar, Gertie, then softened her tone. "We have got to make the most of things, got to get on with our lives. Look at Reenie; she's out having fun and helping people. She's not stuck indoors moping around." Alby knew she was right. They had argued and fought for too long and this war was just another reason for him to lose his rag for no reason, he put his empty cup back on the sideboard and eased himself up out of the chair. He moved towards Gertie with his hands outstretched, embracing; they hugged each other with a warmth and passion that had been missing from their marriage for a long time. They continued to cuddle each other for several minutes and then slowly, Alby stood back from his wife, he gently cupped her face in his wizened old hands making sure he never once stopped looking directly into her eyes as he briefly blinked away a tear.

"You're right Gertie, you always are!" he told her warmly. "But they ain't going to get us down. They ain't heard of our Great British Spirit."

Gertie smiled. She hadn't heard Alby this positive in

years. She stroked his cheek lovingly. "That's better, Alby," she said, happy in the knowledge that he was listening at long last. They continued to talk, standing in the middle of the room, completely lost in each other's passionate embrace.

Gertie spoke warmly and softly as Alby continued to hug his beloved wife. She then stood back and looked deeply into his eyes.

"Alby?" she asked softly. "Do you think you could walk as far as the tube tonight? We may even get a good night's sleep." He smiled and took a few steps towards where his old jacket, that had been rescued from his destroyed house, was hanging on the back of the badly painted blue door. Upon reaching up to retrieve his beloved jacket, he immediately stopped and clamped his hand to his backside. The wound still raw and deep under the layers of bandage was suddenly more than just a little uncomfortable. Pain shot down his right leg accompanied by an awful burning sensation; he winced and doubled up with the pain.

"Ooooh, oooh," he cried, suddenly he felt an overwhelming need to scratch at his leg as the burning sensation started to become more of an irritant.

"Gertie my 'arris don't half itch, love. You wouldn't take a look would you?" Gertie laughed as she put her cable knit back in her canvas bag,

"You're having a laugh." She chuckled.

"I've never been so serious!" Alby was now on his knees his head pressed up hard against the grubby back-room door beads of sweat tumbling down the back of his neck as he raged to himself tearing at his backside through his trousers. "It feels like one of your cable knits has been stitched to me salotch!" he roared. "I didn't like that nurse. I wouldn't put it past her.

she was a nasty piece of work. Oooh, Gertie you gotta have a look, babe," he begged her, she'd seen this before though. It bought a wry smile to her face whenever Alby had a cut finger or squashed his thumb from his handyman exploits, he'd cry like a baby and for all their tenderness earlier, she wasn't going to tend to every one of Alby's problems.

"Look after yourself, Alby. I won't nursemaid you. You brought all this on yourself."

"I know," he said, "but a bit of compassion goes an awfully long way." Alby forced himself back away from the door and tore off his belt, unbuttoned his trousers and pulled them down around his ankles. He then ripped the bandages from around the wound and furiously thrust his hands at the affliction.

"Ooooh, I don't think there's a bit of flesh without a stitch on it." Gertie took her handbag out from under the kitchen table and started to rummage through its contents taking out an old brown bottle stained from years of having its contents spill over its sides. She squinted at the label to read what the bottle held and taking out a very old pair of eyeglasses, she proceeded to read the label. "Let's have a look at what we got then." Smiling to herself, she walked towards the crippled Alby. "What about some of this horse liniment? We've had it for years. Dad used to put it on his farmers. Swore by it, he did."

"Slap it on, love!" Alby yelped almost delirious, she poured a small amount into the palm of her cupped hand.

"Didn't half make him jump though," she said as she slapped it hard, into the inflamed mess of blood and stitches.

Alby's piercing cry could be heard on the roof at St Paul's as once again the fire watchers gathered for another night high up in London's night skies.

***

Mid-day and Charing Cross police station was now buzzing. The weather over central London was bright and clear after a chilly start had brought some light rain whilst those sheltering overnight in the tubes had wound their way home.

PC Selby had two of Ireland's finest banged up in cell number two after he had found them dazed but luckily unhurt amid the debris of the disused tunnel. He had immediately arrested them and charged them with firearms offences amongst many other charges he said he was still mulling over. If he wasn't going to get the spiv, at least he would get the honour of their scalps on his watch. But it had been seven hours since he'd last spoken to them and they had spent that time together in one cell much to his annoyance and when he came back on duty, he let the custody sergeant know how irresponsible it had been to put them together. But with so little space and too few officers on duty, the duty sergeant had no other choice, PC Selby needed to calm himself, tea was the best thing, it was, after all, the start of another long shift and he would need some sustenance to get him through his audience with the two Irish delinquents.

Ardle was pacing up and down cell number two and had been for a full ten minutes since he'd woken from his slumber. The dank cell was small, ten feet across and eight feet six inches long. Ardle had paced it out, his knowledge of measurement picked up from years working on building sites all over Ireland. The window was high up on the far wall and there was very little light coming through it, probably caused by the build-up of dirt and dust that was swirling around the capital after every round of Hitler's bombs that destroyed the surrounding buildings on an increasingly daily basis. Paddy still sitting in one corner with his back propped against the one bed that ran down the left-hand side of the room as you entered it. There was a big metal clank as the key turned and all the tumblers in the lock fell into position on the other side of the door. Paddy immediately sprang to his feet as the big iron door swung into the room. A cold draught from the corridor entered the room and Ardle shivered to himself as two big burly PCs walked into the room. The 'blakeys' in their heels clicking on the cold concrete below as they strode purposefully in.

"Right, you two," said the biggest copper. He looked every inch the part, unlike Gerald, who, whilst he had been a copper for too many years than he cared to mention, he always looked more like someone who was playing at policing rather than one who looked menacing enough to be taken seriously and this one really did look menacing. Paddy cowered as the huge man moved further into the room. "It's alright, young man," he teased Paddy, who in turn tried to make light of his obvious alarm at the man's size.

"Paddy don't go saying anything that'll land us in deep water,"

"We'd be needing that boat again then, Ardle," mused Paddy. Ardle smiled and shook his head at Paddy's attempts at being witty. "If you say so, Paddy."

As the two men were ushered from the cell and out into the cold corridor, they caught sight of Gerald stood near the sergeant's desk, sipping on a cup of tea. They both gave him a smile and a wink as he shook his head towards them both. After a few more twists, turns and stairways around the police station, they were both shown into a large room with a desk in the middle. Obviously, it had been set up for them as it had two hard chairs on one side and just one slightly more padded one on the other side of the desk. Paddy, oblivious to what was going on, sat in the single chair until Ardle firmly gave him a clip to his ear and nodded towards the chairs on the other side. Paddy raised his eyebrows in mock horror at his mistake. Both men sat down and the huge policemen left the room shutting the door firmly behind him. There was a single light suspended from the high ceiling on a long curly brown wire. A horde of spiders had made their webs along its length, cascading down onto the top of the yellowing shade that was slung above the bulb. There were no windows in this room, and it smelt of a thousand men and women's confessions. They sat in silence for a while before Ardle broke the peace.

"Remember," said Ardle.

"What?" Paddy was confused again.

"Oh bloody hell!" The two men had just started a conversation when Gerald entered purposefully. He'd left the men to sweat for ten minutes. Confidently, he strode over to the table, put a file of paper and some pencils down and then stood back eyeing the two men with suspicion. A broad smile traced its way across Gerald's small features.

"So," he said to the two Irishmen, clapping his hands together in glee, "caught in the act, trapped as well. Made it easy for us, didn't you?"

Ardle saw a chance to turn on the charm. "Ah…this could be your lucky night officer; do you have a wife? Of cou…"

"Oh don't start all that," Gerald cut in without giving

Ardle the chance to finish his sentence.

"That was bloody stupid, Ardle." Paddy was now cross himself. They both sat there with their hands in their pockets looking at the floor, waiting for Gerald to really put the boot in.

"Ardle...Ardle Conlan." Gerald thought he would try the nice policeman approach hoping that a gentle voice used with a small amount of persuasion would have the desired effect. "Are you going to tell me what you were doing in the underground when the tunnel collapsed?"

Paddy couldn't resist. "We were on a sponsored walk, Officer."

Slapping him hard across the top of his legs, Ardle whispered to Paddy to shut his mouth. "We weren't on a sponsored walk, Officer. I made that bit up!" said Paddy, wincing from the pain caused by Ardle's aggressiveness.

"You surprise me!" Gerald said nonchalantly. Both men sat again in stony silence. Both trying to decide how much they should or shouldn't say to get themselves out of the situation. Ardle was the first to be heard above the large ticking clock positioned for maximum effect over the door facing both the men.

"I'll be honest, Officer. We were a bit off the beaten track. The fact of the matter is we were looking for the drains." Amused, Gerald reminded them that they were caught two hundred feet down in a closed-off part of the underground system.

"Was it closed off?" Paddy felt he needed to offer some sort of intelligent comment and looked at Ardle for some encouragement, not to be beaten though, Ardle decided it was time he played his trump card. He'd known all along that if things became sticky, reminding Gerald what they had seen might just get them out of anything difficult, but he also knew it had to be played correctly in an assured way leaving Gerald no other option. He started to sow the seeds.

"We just followed your man in."

"Our man?" confused, Gerald asked Ardle whether he would like to elaborate.

"Would we like to do what, Officer?" Paddy inquired. Ardle looked at Paddy, his eyes piercing deep into Paddy's, but Paddy gave him his, 'leave this to me' look and so Ardle sat back, sighing to himself, praying that Paddy wouldn't drop them further into the mire.

"Elaborate!" Gerald said once more gesturing to them both; once more Paddy shook his head.

"I'm not sure what you mean."

Taking his seat across the table from the two Irishmen, Gerald eyed them both warily. They were either playing with him or they were both incredibly stupid and he needed to find out one way or the other, fast. He put both his hands on the table took a deep breath and looked across at them through gritted teeth.

"The man who is he?" he asked, almost begging them to come clean so he could get this over with.

"We don't know, Officer," Ardle replied, Gerald bit his lip and visibly slumped back in his chair, he was being taken for a mug he thought.

He tried again. "So you followed someone, who you had no idea who he was, into an area of the underground system and just happened to get trapped. So where was he when the station collapsed?" Gerald knew no one else had been found in the tunnel after they'd cleared up so Ardle must have been

185

lying. Ardle knew better.

"I don't know, but what I do know is he helped the children out a bit later on."

Gerald lent back in his chair and scratched his head. "So he was there when it collapsed?" he asked.

"Oh no just us and the children." Gerald was getting confused. "So why haven't the children said anything about you then?"

"They didn't know we were there either," Paddy spoke up still rubbing his stinging thigh.

Getting to his feet, Gerald paced around the room trying to make sense of what had been said, who was the mystery man? It still hadn't dawned on Gerald they were talking about Ralph.

"So what were you doing there?" This time, he came across with a much sterner attitude and there was a long pause before Paddy spoke to Gerald and as he did so, a huge grin creased his dirty stubbly cheeks.

"Would you like some chocolate?" he asked as he reached into the depths of his jacket to fetch out a tattered bar of something that used to resemble a bar of chocolate.

"No, I don't want any bloody chocolate!" Gerald shouted angrily back.

"Well, it seems, we're in a bit of a deadlock here then," Ardle spoke in an assured tone. "After all, did you know what was in there when you and your man came to a bit of an agreement?" The Irishman hit Gerald right between the eyes and Gerald knew it. He coughed and spluttered at the thought of his prized catch getting one over on him.

Trying to defend himself, limply, he simply replied, "I don't know what you mean." Beaming from ear-to-ear, Ardle knew his trump card was now well and truly laid.

"Then perhaps, I better elaborate," he said chuckling to himself.

"Your man…the spiv guy, the one you introduced to your good lady."

"That's the one," Paddy joined in, revelling in their newfound powers of persuasion. "Oh and she spent the night with him as well." The veins in Gerald's neck pulsed. The spiv had got to him again and he wasn't even in the room. Gerald was ready to explode, visibly shaking, he sat back down and shuffled the paperwork in front of him and made a few notes with one of the little grey pencils lying on the table.

"It's been a long night," he said. "So you were looking for the drains?"

"That we were," Ardle proudly responded.

"Were we?" said a confused Paddy. Ardle shut him up quickly.

"To repair the broken sewerage system and your tools?" Gerald was now offering them a polite and easy get out of jail card.

"They got lost when it all collapsed," Ardle assured him; clasping his hands together as in victory Gerald smiled and told them both that, actually all appeared well.

There was a brief moment as Ardle and Paddy took in what Gerald had just said. Stunned, both the Irishmen looked at each other, wary of Gerald and what had just happened. They quickly rose from their chairs and rushed round the table as fast as they could to congratulate Gerald on his decision.

"Ah, you're a fair man, officer," said Ardle, "but I'd have a word with that harlot of a wife of yours."

"Aye," said Paddy. "She likes far too much chocolate!"

Gerald spun the big old key in the lock until a distinctive clunk was heard, turning the handle clockwise he opened the door and gestured the men to leave.

"Go…just go," he said. Both men rushed past Gerald and out into the dimly lit corridor as Gerald returned to the table, sitting, he buried his head into his folded arms as they rest on the old table in front of him, sure the water that pooled in the corner of his eyes was from the stuffy atmosphere there in the basement and not for any other reason.

***

People had started to gather at the Aldwych early in the afternoon. They'd heard that tonight there was going to be a party in the station and that Ralph and Charlie were guests of honour. Long lines of blue, white, and red bunting had been strung in the entrance archways and huge union jacks proudly hung from every available position. All day the regular commuters had been asked to make a contribution towards the party and many had put hard-earned cash into a tin, or donated things, hard to find things, to be made up into delicious party food for those evening celebrations. Many of the hotels in the area had heard of Ralphs exploits and had also donated, especially The Savoy Hotel upon The Strand. They had given several plates of cooked meat and Victor had stored them in a cold place safely in his office under wraps until they were to be needed later. A really long table had been set up on the platform almost eighty feet from one end to the other a bit wobbly in places and some parts higher than others, many of the women who had been sheltering in the station over the last few weeks had been busy trying to find enough table clothes to cover it in.

The station platform had been transformed from a gloomy, dank, grey tunnel and all the glossy tiles that ran the length of the platform had been polished until they shone in the low lights up and down the station, after they too had also been cleaned of all their year's grime.

More lengths of bunting had been strung up all the way down the stairway and Union Jacks had been suspended over the advertising posters up and down the station concourse.

Winnie was particularly grateful, especially to Ralph, so she'd quickly got herself over to 'G. Kelly's Noted Eel and Pie shop' in Bow that morning and had persuaded them to deliver a huge amount of jellied eels and pie and mash to adorn the table for the party-goers in the evening. True to his word, Ralph had been to see many of his less salubrious business partners and throughout the day, various crates of beer had been delivered to the station from Charringtons, Wandsworth and Wenlocks and more besides, all with Ralphs name on them. Soon, Victor's office was more like the bar of a public house. Beer and snacks were piled wherever a place could be found for them to be stored safely, including the trays of meat and sandwiches that had been delivered from Smithfield's. Everybody there was kept busy, cleaning and polishing, sweeping, and dusting until the place looked like a new penny. Victor had never seen his station look so grand and as he proudly walked around it on his evening's inspection. The hairs on the back of his neck craned themselves over his collar as his sense of pride burst forth everywhere he looked.

At exactly six o clock that evening, all the food and drink was brought carefully from Victor's office and laid neatly on the tables down on the bright and gay platform by the many people already gathered there to greet the evening's guests of honour. Tim, who was standing near the platform entrance eyeing up the Cockney delicacies, had never seen such food before.

The old piano that Ralph and Charlie had seen in the disused tunnel had been cleaned and tuned by one of London's finest and had been placed with precision in the middle of the platform.

The place was awash with so many people who had all heard about Ralph and Charlie's exploits the previous evening and they wanted to make sure that both men were honoured in the best way imaginable, the London Way. Pearly Kings and Queens from all over the Capital gathered in their glittering costumes and soon, the piano was belting out its first tune as they all rowdily sang 'My old mans a dustman' which could be heard up in the entrance to the Aldwych just as Ralph and Reenie were being dropped off at the entrance by one of London's black cabs. Punctual as ever, Ralph appeared first with Reenie taking his right arm as she too stepped from the vehicle. They had both spent the afternoon with Connie and Charlie. Connie had made sure that Reenie was elegantly attired in a beautiful blue and white lace fronted full-length dress with strikingly high shoes to match, a stole had been carefully placed over her shoulders to keep the evenings chill at bay. Ralph had changed from his working suit into a beautifully tailored dinner jacket and matching trousers with bright shiny patent black shoes, his hair firmly fixed into place with a large handful of Brylcreem.

Connie and Charlie followed from the cab. Connie, as elegant as ever, was impeccably turned out and proudly gripped Charlie as they stepped forward towards the station's entrance. Charlie had made a more modest attempt and his version of best dressed was to keep his clothes to his normal attire with the one exception, the creases in his sleeves and trouser legs were as sharp as a razor's edge as if he had spent all day with an iron before he dressed for the big night. Winnie quickly fell in behind Charlie from where she had been stood, waiting with Alice, making last-minute arrangements with some other local cabbies to ferry all the children from the hospital to join them all.

As the first cabs with the children appeared in the street, Alice and Connie descended the stairs and made their way towards the platform followed by Reenie and Ralph. Charlie entered with Winnie proudly holding his arm, as they stepped onto the platform Charlie yelled, "The children are coming!" at everyone.

Winnie and the other mothers waited eagerly for them to step from the cabs and descend into the Aldwych.

The kids had all been cleaned up and they had all been given shiny new shoes by a local shoe shop to go with the new jumpers and shorts; and dresses for the girls which had all been donated by the big hotel up on The Strand. Josey, his leg covered in a huge cast made of plaster, limped on an old wooden crutch, Winnie looked proudly on at her boy.

"These rascals. Do you know how long they have been running wild around these tunnels without us knowing? It's been a blooming disaster waiting to happen if our Charlie hadn't been on hand," she said to Reenie as they entered the platform area.

"It wasn't your Charlie that saved these children though was it. No, it was my Ralph." Reenie was still not happy with

191

Winnie, and she was certainly not going to let Charlie take the credit for rescuing the children when it was Ralph who had managed to get them out without any further damage to them.

"Your Ralph? You're married to a copper." Winnie cut back snidely "Was!". Reenie told her as she snuggled up to the large man who stood proudly next to her.

"I'm fed-up living hand to mouth, and this man has shown me that you can have fun and live a little even if there is a war on."

"Have you told him yet?" Winnie questioned Reenie. She'd spied Gerald at the far end of the platform, surrounded by other policemen and some of the local dignitaries and was sure it would all blow up if they didn't manage to keep each other apart.

"Told who?" Reenie asked.

"Your old man, you soppy mare. I'm sure he'll have something to say about it."

Reenie didn't care. She was totally lost in her newfound romance with Ralph and made sure she told everyone who could hear that it was 'none of their business' if she was having a bit of fun with Ralph, even if it cost her marriage.

"Now clear off and leave me alone!" she spat at Winnie. Spotting Gertie and Alby near the piano, she made her excuses and left them all, tugging at Ralph to follow her along the platform. They both swiftly made their way towards the centre of the station, passing Gerald about halfway along. They briefly stopped and Reenie urged Gerald to be happy for her, Ralph shook the PC's hand before they moved away with no more being said. Alice, who was stood near to Gerald and the other dignitaries, could see the old copper was heartbroken and rushing to his side, she offered him her condolences, falling on deaf ears Gerald was a broken man and quietly, he left the station. Parties weren't his thing!

But tonight wasn't about him or his marriage or about Ralph or even about surviving Hitler's bombers. Tonight was going to be party a night to celebrate.

They weren't going to be beaten.

God Save the King.